In the game of Love

One step forward Two steps back...

Meenakshi Kumar

Vitasta
Let Knowledge Spread

Published by
Renu Kaul Verma
Vitasta Publishing Pvt Ltd
2/15, Ansari Road, Daryaganj
New Delhi-110 002
info@vitastapublishing.com

ISBN 978-93-86473-06-6

First Edition 2017
Second Reprint 2019
MRP ₹ 295

Disclaimer
All persons portrayed in this book are fictitious. Any resemblance to real persons, living or dead, is purely co-incidental. Though this is a work of fiction, opinions expressed in it are the author's own. The publisher is in no way responsible for these.

Cover and layout by Vits Press
Printed by Vikas Computer and Printers

Dedication

To the Almighty and the memory of my father
Shri A K Varma and father-in-law Dr Kameshwar

What should we write
on the immaculate hearts &
minds of all cherubs, so dear!

Of course, a story of
Love, care & affection
and not despair.

For every society
will have to live tomorrow
the story it writes today!

Acknowledgement

Thanks to my darling sons, Shreyash and Divyesh, for being my greatest support, and to the backbone of our family, Sandeep, my husband.

I want to thank my mom Neelam Varma for being the tender but tenacious shield that protected me and helped me to strengthen my identity in this world.

My heartfelt thanks to Sajal Srivastava, my friend from Shaheed Sukhdev College of Business Studies, for providing the much needed succour with his encouraging words.

When I thought that my work was over, it was not! And, for this I would like to thank Ms Sonalini Chaudhary, and Mr Anuj Bahari from Red Ink Literary Agency for their valuable inputs.

My sincerest thanks to Ms Renu Kaul Verma, Managing Director, Vitasta publishing for her support. I would like to specially thank my editor, Ms Veena Batra, for the meticulous editing of the manuscript. And also the entire team at Vitasta for doing a wonderful job.

Finally, I want to thank all my readers who alone would have the final say in framing the destiny of this book.

ONE

SUMAN SAT BESIDE Rajan on a couch in the lobby of Star International Hotel. They were waiting for their very important NRI clients to arrive. As the two glanced at their watches almost simultaneously, they knew the guests, along with senior officials of their company, would be there any minute. Though guests occupy an important place in Indian tradition, these NRI guests or clients actually meant a great deal for the company's growth chart. Suman and Rajan, deputed for the arrangements, had been on their toes finalizing all the preparations for the day's meeting. Suman's searching eyes, focussed on the hotel's opulent entrance suddenly saw someone that made her fair complexion change to a bright angry red. Her pretty pink mouth wore a sneer that would have translated into the choicest abuse had she gathered herself enough to vent her emotions.

She raised herself from her seat with agility, as if apprehending an impending attack, and started walking towards the hotel entrance with hurried steps, without a care for the spectacle she would make if she tripped on the longish hem of her sari.

Needless to say, her sudden prance had confounded Rajan. He, too, stood up in response to her reaction. His forehead crinkled as his brown eyes widened behind the black-rimmed spectacles. He made an effort to follow her. But before Rajan could even move outside the couch area, Suman halted, retraced her steps and came back to her seat. Like a lost soul, she dumped herself most inelegantly on the couch again.

'What happened to you Suman?' asked Rajan in a questioning voice. This was completely unlike the proper and efficiently in-control Suman he knew.

Suman said in a low voice, her head leaning back on the couch, 'I missed getting the scoundrel!'

'Who...Suman? Whom are you talking about?' asked Rajan with emphasis this time.

Suman gestured towards the main entrance of the hotel, from where a couple was moving out of the gate. Her eyes were still agitated as she saw their backs moving out of sight.

Rajan looking puzzled asked, 'But why are you so worked up, Suman! Did they do any wrong to you?' Then he smiled and added on a lighter note, 'It seems you have had a nightmare about these people.'

'Nightmare! No, daymare!' Suman said tightening her lips, her voice a shrill whisper, seething with barely controlled anger.

'Daymare! But why? And is that even a thing? Why should a stranger make you have the DAYMARE?' Rajan looked bemusedly at a visibly chagrined Suman. 'It seems you lost sleep last night in anticipation of today's meeting…are you going to be alright?'

His constant questioning and confusion just served to irritate Suman further.

'You keep making fun of me.' Suman was tearful this time. 'Why aren't you taking me seriously? I wonder why I would need enemies when blessed with a friend like you!'

Rajan knew by now that there was something terribly wrong that was disturbing Suman so much. He placed his hand on hers, contrite, and said, 'I was trying to make the situation less tense so that you don't appear stressed to our senior management team.'

'Rajan,' Suman said, 'I fear for my cousin. The couple that I was pointing at is known to me. And the cause of concern is that I have just seen my cousin in the arms of a man who is a big cheat!'

Before Suman could explain further, she saw their MD leading the guests towards them.

They both stood up and Rajan murmured, 'Suman, just simmer down; after we are through with the meeting we will go to a coffee shop and then we can talk over your issues in detail. I'm sure we both together will be able to find a solution to your problem. For now, just relax and look cool or else this meeting will go for a toss.'

Suman tried to look cheerful and walked behind Rajan to greet the guests.

The meeting ended on a positive note. The itinerary for the guests was finalized, and thereafter, the guests took leave to relax in their rooms. The MD congratulated Rajan and Suman for making such excellent arrangements for the day, and bade them goodbye. Suman and Rajan decided to drive to a nearby coffee shop.

She had still not recovered from the incident at the hotel. She looked worried. Her face bore a morose look, a helpless frown marking her forehead. After a brief spell of stillness that perturbed Rajan all the more, he broke the silence.

'Suman, until and unless you share your problem, you will not be able to have a restful sleep at night, and you know the amount of pressure we need to take in coming days to make our international project a success.'

Looking at Rajan, Suman thanked her stars for having him in her life. What a wonderful, calming man,wanting to share her worries with him, Suman was transported back to the time where it had all begun.

TWO

SLOGGING DAY IN and day out, preparing for the entrance examination, was not as torturous as waiting for the results. Since the due date of result announcement was already over, the waiting caused greater anxiety and despair. The mornings began with hope, but ended in angst. Suman had worked hard for the examination, but its result was beyond her control. A seat in a reputed business school could mean a breakthrough in her career graph and establish her on the path to success.

She paced the distance from her room to the entrance door, not one or two, but umpteen times. Her every task was interspersed by checking, yet again, the door entrance. Tired of her to and fro motion, which had become a daily ritual, she sat beside the window. She stared listlessly at the clouds playing the game of hide and seek with the earth; dark clouds would come and go and the concurrent dust storms with thundering nebula raised hopes of rain to give respite from the sweltering heat. The earth would become hopeful at the sight of clouds, the clouds would then hide behind the hot sun and once again, poor earth would have to fall back on patience and faith. She wondered about how closely this game of the elements of nature matched with her own wait and patience.

Savita, Suman's mother, looked for Suman all around the house, and finally came to check Suman's favourite place. Suman sat beside the window, her eyes searching the sky above.

Suman's pleadings to be left to her own devices had never worked well with her mother. Savita was annoyed and worried at her daughter's restiveness, and pushed her to accompany her to the market to run some errands. It wasn't like Savita thought that the teeming masses of humanity, the sweltering heat, commotion and noise of the local market would give her daughter any pleasure. But she was a staunch believer in retail therapy, and if nothing, Suman would at least be distracted from her turmoil.

The market was full of people, a rainbow of varied shades and emotions that made up this mankind. Shopping, perhaps, is one activity that rouses a person to complete alertness, curiosity, and high levels of enthusiastic energy. People all around haggled with vendors to strike the best deal. The cacophony of vendors and customers sounded like the crackling of an ancient sound system needing repair.

The foodies flocked around streetfood stalls. Girls giggled and ladies stood gossiping and laughing in long serpentine queues before the *golgappa* seller, holding on to their plates, waiting for their turn to devour a serving of mouth-watering golgappas. Others relished aloo tikkis with colourful, green and red chutney, smooth white curd and ground spices. The wide-mouthed Indian wok, more than half full of oil, contained rounds of wriggly lines forming into hard crust jalebis; the man clenching the cloth holding batter, rotated his hands like an artist holds his brush to paint the canvas with his strokes. After dropping the jalebi rounds in the wok, he picked them up, immersed them in the sugar syrup and heaped them on the perforated spatula to let the extra juice drip back into the hot syrup.

The delicious aroma wafting through the air had the power to trigger the most dormant appetites, but not so in the case of Suman. Despite her mother's insistence, she did not want to eat any of her favorite food. Watching happy faces of people glued to the food stalls, having satiated their gastronomical gluttony, could hold her attention only briefly.

Savita was holding Suman's hand in a firm clasp like she

did when Suman was a child and navigated the stone hewed narrow pathways of the bazaar, like a cork bobbing up and down flowing with the stream of humanity, caught up for a while against the kiosks and then drawn away by the flowing current. Suman's senses had started drowning in the chaos of the market, her mind still glued to the entrance of her home. She wanted to rush back to reach her home. And she raced through the market leaving her mother behind to find a rickshaw to drop them to their residence.

All through the fifteen minutes ride on the rickshaw, Suman kept biting her nails. Savita had to reprimand her constantly, warning her, 'Suman my darling, nothing except patience will help you. Your nails will start bleeding if you chew them like this!' But it was difficult for Suman to keep still. As soon as the rickshaw came near her house, she jumped off, and rushed to their mailbox. She opened it to check if there was any letter for them.

'Yes…!'

There was the envelope for which she had been waiting. It had the emblem of the Indian Institute of Management, Ahmedabad, and was addressed in her name. Her heart started pounding. It was difficult to get inside the house and open the letter. She could not wait a moment longer, and with thousand butterflies in her stomach, she started to tear the seal of the envelope.

A few drops of water fell on her face, hands, and on the envelope; her anxiety changed to an inexplicable anger! The water droplets served the purpose of fat used to increase the intensity of fire.

She looked up confident that the kids residing on the top floor were playing pranks on her by throwing water. They had done this earlier, but only when the Holi festival was round the corner. She had never become angry with them. She had dealt with their mischief with a smile and a warning to not get them sweets. This time, it was different.

She muttered, 'Enough is enough; my goodness! Why can't the parents teach their kids to behave properly?'

But she could see no one above. She looked from different angles to check for a human form, but no, there was nobody hiding.

And then her eyes shifted to look at the sky above; like we seek an answer to everything beyond our perceptible limits by looking up, believing that there resides an unknown power, an unlimited source of energy.

Suman got the answer, as a few more drops had fallen on her by that time.

Yes! Indeed, it was raining!

'Wow!' she exclaimed.

Savita reached her with racing steps and asked, 'What has happened, Suman?'

'It's raining! It's raining, Mom!'

Savita smiled at Suman's exultation at the sight of rain.

'Suman you are behaving like a child,' she said, shifting her gaze to the envelope in Suman's hand. 'Whose letter is this?'

Her mother's question brought Suman's attention back to the letter. Rather than replying to her, she rushed inside her house. Savita followed her closing the door and by the time she turned to look at Suman and repeat her question, Suman was reading the letter with a grin on her face.

She could easily read the expression on her daughter's face. It was the look of success! Joy and pride oozed from her face. She went near her daughter, kissed her forehead and embraced her in a tight hug.

Suman's eyes welled up with tears and in a choked voice she said, 'I have done it, Mom! IIM Ahmedabad, my dream destination!'

The few drops of trickling raindrops had changed to a happy, hearty shower.

Suman's happiness knew no bounds and nature seemed to complement her feeling The land had become parched due to the heat for days. The unexpected showers made the whole civilization dance to the tune of happiness and life. The raindrops breathed energy into vegetation, which was on the verge of collapse. The rain seeped through cracks and fissures and the air absorbed the aroma of the soil and emanated as fresh earth fragrance. It made the air refreshing, like the ecstatic smile of a newly-wed bride, waiting for her husband to return after a long day of work.

The fervour in nature was transmitted to the animals and the vegetation alike. The gusts of wind accompanying the rain blew through bushes and trees making them dance elatedly. The stray animals also rejoiced at the sight.

Suman was standing in the corner of the verandah collecting raindrops in her cupped hands. She had closed her eyes to let the coolness soak in to reach her soul.

After a long time, she was experiencing the bliss of a child—carefree and relaxed. She wanted to jump and play with the rainwater, but biologically she had crossed the boundaries of her childhood, and hence, was too old for such an activity. But, her spirits danced within her. She felt on cloud nine.

THREE

IIM AHMEDABAD! SHE was finally here. Feet firmly planted on terra firma, bags in tow and all the belongings she needed to see her through the haloed corridors of this prestigious institute.

Before entering the reception, Suman looked all around to take in her surroundings. Her ears could hear her heart thumping to a loud, excited beat; she took a deep breath to calm down. But before she could get an adequate hold on her composure, she bumped into, probably, the hottest looking girl at the IIM campus. The girl was dressed to tease, it seemed. She wore extremely snug denim capris and a red tee shirt with a neckline that plunged so low it left hardly anything to imagination. Her fair complexion and masses of messed up wavy hair flying in the breeze made her look like Venus reclining by the wall! When, as a girl, Suman had such a strong reaction, she didn't need to look around to see what was happening to the boys.

The girl stood leaning against the wall across from the entrance of the reception hall, one pedicured foot against the wall; the other resting on the marble floor, putting to shame the marble, with its glowing pristine fairness. She chewed gum as she closely scrutinized all the entrants.

It was difficult for people entering the gate to ignore her presence, both due to her looks and the place she had stationed herself. For a few seconds, Suman's gaze stayed glued to the girl, but then she moved on to the admission counter. Such eye candies were of no interest to her.

She reported at the admission counter. After completing the formalities, Suman picked up her bag to quickly get to her allotted room, but her attempt was foiled. She heard someone call out her name and turned to answer.

'Hi!'

The girl had walked the distance from the wall to the counter and stood behind Suman. She extended her hand in greeting.

'My name is Arunima! I am your roommate.'

And the sentences followed one after another, like an express train with no stoppage!

'Call me Anu! Why waste time in a long introduction

when we can get things done in a lesser time.'

Quite logical! Suman thought.

There was no sign of Arunima ending her monologue, but Suman was tired and wanted to relax. She tried to take leave of her room partner by trying to explain that she was tired, but to say something to Arunima was like trying to get into a running bus and falling flat on the face.

Suman had yet to decide how to move away, when another surprising reaction jolted her. Arunima held her at arm's distance, inspecting her like she had chanced upon a rare specimen of wildlife. She let out a low whistle of surprise!

'It appears I have gone back to primitive times. Did you get your clothes from a museum, girl?'

Arunima's face bore a look of great amusement.She looked almost like those foreigners touring Indian villages and marvelling at how primitive things were. Suman was not one to take to this fashion policing kindly, though she was taken unawares. And she had not quite expected it in a place like IIM, where clearly it was brains that got one a place rather than beauty.

So she squared her shoulders, stood her ground and defended her elegant salwar kurta with great aplomb and just the right tinge of sarcasm. 'It's called a salwar kurta, my dear. Pity you haven't seen one before.... You see how it's serving the purpose of clothing me than what little bit you have on.'

Suman felt shaken to the core. She had never been judged like this. But she had to exercise restraint. She took a deep breath and pretended to look comfortable. She looked around to check if anyone had noticed them or overheard their exchange. She did not want to appear a fool to passers-by. Suman was wearing a round necked printed full sleeve kurta, reaching a little below her knees, a white salwar and a white dupatta. The dress, though not the latest in fashion, was traditional, elegant and what she was most comfortable in. She had never needed to defend her style or lack of it before. She was nonplussed but ready to take it on.

She threw a resentful glance at Arunima and said, 'And I think you should mind your own business.' Then Suman tried to rush off, tightening her grip on the bag handle.

'Hey! Wait up! I didn't mean to hurt your feelings… believe me, I did not mean this at all!' Arunima rushed blabbering behind Suman.

'You are looking so graceful in your attire. It's just that I have not worn a salwar kurta ever, but mind you I should like to borrow yours sometime to check whether I also look as pretty and graceful as you do!'

Suman was puzzled! She didn't know how to react. But, Arunima's honest confession made her mood take an about turn and she could not help smiling when the girl said, 'Hey I just wanted to become familiar with you before we share our room. In fact, I was quite restless to know about my roommate, and now I know it is you!'

Suman's only option was to calm down and let it go. It was then that she got a chance to speak and she could ask, 'How do you know that we are roommates?'

'Just wait for a while.'

Suman too could hear the man sitting at the reception counter announcing room numbers. Arunima smiled and added, 'I hope you know that two people are supposed to share one room.' Suman nodded.

'I am the first occupant of my room and today being the last day of reporting, I was sure that the other occupant would join soon.So I waited here at the counter to welcome my room partner. In fact, I know the rooms of many of our classmates,' Arunima said laughingly, her face and behavior showing no trace of grudge despite Suman's belligerence a few moments ago.

Suman could not help feeling amused.

The two girls walked towards their room hanging their bags on their shoulders, discussing their background and the anxiety they had waiting for their final result from the institute.

By the time they reached their room, Suman had changed her opinion about Arunima. The silver lining about Arunima's personality was that she had her heart in the right place. In a time where femininity is more about flaunting ones sexuality by revealing more skin, it was forgivable that someone had reacted with such surprise and insensitivity at a traditional attire that seemed to be soon becoming a relic of the past. Girls like Suman, who valued traditions, morals and a certain modesty as their prized possessions were soon fading into oblivion.

FOUR

SUMAN'S BELONGINGS CONSISTED of just a suitcase, and a duffel bag with things that could comfortably be set in half of the cupboard allotted to her. To believe the same of Arunima was difficult, because their hostel room looked like a cluttered barn, full of latest electronic gadgets, designer clothes, expensive cosmetics and fashion magazines. The entire room was full of Arunima's things. The room looked unique as all other rooms were full of books and this appeared like a discotheque in the middle of the vast temple-like complex.

Despite making the best possible use of their time management lesson, the students were not able to handle the stress of the course. There was always a time crunch to cope with lessons along with routine activities. The students reached the class with ruffled hair, sleepy eyes,wearing a distressed look because of compromising with at least one of the essential rituals; sleep or breakfast or bath. Those who could make themselves look a little presentable would often fight a losing battle with sleep in the class. They would doze off right under the professor's nose.

Everyone was part of the race to perform better than the other; the frantic page turning for scoring in the quizzes, straining eyes reading small fonts of lengthy readings for the class, and other struggles and scuffles required to get a good grade. Arunima, on the contrary, looked cool and contented fiddling around with her gadgets, or flipping through her favorite fashion magazine, or listening to the latest numbers on her iPod.

She always sat in the last corner seat of the class, where she could evade being spotted by the professors. The warnings by professors were as ineffective as water off a duck's back. Most of the times, she kept doodling on blank pages and disturbed even those who, unfortunately, had occupied the seat next to her.

Suman would, at times, become quite surprised at Arunima's indifferent attitude. After all, she must have put in efforts like everyone! They had literally won a war on the battlefield of their career by clearing the IIM entrance, then why was Arunima so callous towards her success! If she did not mend her ways, she might have to face expulsion from the institute. She thought that as a friend she had a duty to at least talk to her and know the reason for her attitude.

And one day, when Arunima seemed in one of her good moods, Suman asked her, 'Hey Anu, I'm sure you must have worked hard to crack the entrance exam, but why do you act like a fish out of water here? It's just a matter of two years, and with all the days already spent, even less than two years in which we can embellish our resume with the degree of this Institute. Rather than wasting your time why don't you do some serious study so that you get out respectably from here?'

Arunima turned her face towards Suman and paused briefly, looking into her eyes; maybe, she was trying to judge the depth of Suman's feelings for her. 'Suman, in my life, till date, I have not found any one so concerned for me!' And she started speaking in a way she had never done before. So profound, so grave that it was difficult to believe it was her.

'Suman, I had never been into serious studies. From the day I realized my identity as a human being, I was in a boarding; of course the best boarding school in the country. My long vacations were spent at my friend's house instead of my own, because my so-called home is just a beautiful building with costly décor, precious decoratives and a lavish ambience. My parents were always busy with either their meetings or parties. If ever they happened to be together it was more like the opposition meeting the ruling party during assembly session, where there is nothing except hatred for each other. It was just because my best friend was preparing for CAT so I also started preparing with her. It was her bad luck that she couldn't get through and my lucky stars worked for me and I am here with you today.'

Suman finally knew the truth about Arunima. She saw her vulnerable side, which was sensitive and insecure. A little prodding was needed to bring out her real self. Suman could feel the child within Arunima, craving for genuine affection. Behind the madness of her wild and carefree look, she had very basic needs of love and security lying unfulfilled. Suman decided to help her friend in whatever way she could.

'Anu, God forbid, had you not managed a seat in this institute, it would have gone to another deserving aspirant. So, enjoy the gift of your destiny and make full use of it by at least clearing your terms with decent grades.' These words from Suman made a serious impact on Arunima. And that was the day she threw away her magazines, cigarette boxes, and pointless gadgetry to replace them with her academic books. This led to two strong foundations; first was of their deep bond of friendship, and second was a good academic record for Arunima.

The litmus test, the first semester exams, approached like dragons making everyone quake in their boots. Arunima needed to put in extra effort to compensate for the initial loss. Suman tried to help her in all possible ways, and the two friends kept their noses to the grindstone. Despite burning the midnight oil, they were finding some topics difficult to grasp. Here, Arunima's PR skills came in handy. Her domain of friendship extended to the entire institute including the boys' dorm.

When both Suman and Arunima failed to solve a numerical that was marked important for the exam, the only option was to take someone's help. After much deliberation, Arunima decided to do something. Grabbing hold of Suman's hand, she pulled her towards the library where most of the boys studied all through the night. While walking past the area separating the boys' and girls' dorms they saw a figure in the dark seeming to be wiping tears from his cheeks. Suman hesitated, but Arunima pulled her near the figure. It was none other than Ritwik, the most brilliant guy in their group. Ritwik was a sweet-natured person who was ready to help anyone in need. 'Hey Ritwik, what's the matter?' Arunima asked.

Ritwik was caught unawares and he turned to face Suman and Arunima, trying to look normal.

'Ritwik, why do you look upset? What's the matter? Is everything ok…?'asked Arunima, worried at his state.

Ritwik tried to dodge the question and said, 'Yeah…

yeah! Everything is fine! It was just a bout of nostalgic feeling!' he said trying to force a smile on his face.

'Hey buddy, you can't fool us like this!' Arunima said. 'Tell us what the matter is? I know you will not shed tears just because you are missing home. Or, may be your mom didn't teach you that boys don't cry…huh!' Arunima said, trying to lighten the mood.

But this humour did not make Ritwik smile. He looked sadder. But just when he was about to give into her entreaties, a message flashed on his cellphone. It was his sister…wishing him a happy birthday. The foxy Arunima had peeped and read the message. 'So, it's your b'day tomorrow, I mean today, because it is already one am,'she said chuckling.

'But still, I cannot understand the cause of your blues, why should somebody be sad on their b'day?' she said, tapping her finger on her cheek, as if she was trying to get hold of some big clue. And then she jumped up closing her open fist as if she had caught hold of a butterfly in the air and said, 'You must be missing the fun at your b'day party at home! But why worry when your friend Arunima is here!' she went on with a glow of victory on her face as if she had found the reason for Ritwik's unhappiness. 'We will celebrate your birthday with all shenanigans included. Come on, cheer up now!' And she patted Ritwik's back like he was just a sulking child.

'Oh come on, Arunima! It's not like I am five and dying for a birthday bash…'Ritwik did not appreciate Arunima making light of his worries.

'Then come on tell us the truth! What's the matter that has made you so upset?'

Ritwik then told them his story…of disillusionment and heartbreak….

He had fallen in love with a girl during graduation. They had made promises to be together in all circumstances. But, last week, one of his friends who also knew his girlfriend, informed him that he had seen her moving around with a rich guy from their town. When Ritwik called her to find out the truth she said that she had made up her mind to settle down with that guy, who could afford to give her all luxuries in life. She preferred to live her dream life—a life full of luxury and comforts with a rich spouse than living a middle class life with him. She had forgotten all her promises for the sake of money.

'I can't believe it! How can anyone do like this?'

'Ritwik,' continued Arunima bemusedly, 'I don't understand how people's minds work? I mean how can one put a price tag on rare attributes like true love? I pity her! My friend, you too should move on. You can't let your life take a pause because of a person who does not know your worth.'

Suman who had not spoken much, added, 'Ritwik may

be you deserve a better partner. I think your girlfriend will repent her decision quite soon. So, don't worry.'

Talking his heart out with the ladies and their words of compassion had the effect of a soothing balm and changed Ritwik's mood for the better.

Only three days were left for the exams, but Arunima planned a small secret party for Ritwik's birthday. She could convince everyone in her dorm and Ritwik's dorm, to manage a few moments from their over packed schedule, for a fun filled celebration.

The activity based on the theme "heartbreak", had most students narrating their encounter with crushes.The confessions of young hearts about their secret dates and the heartbreaks, while having a rendezvous with infatuation made others feel a bit lighter.

Only a few were the lucky souls to have their relationships still carrying on, whereas some were still on the way to find a dream mate. The session was quite enlightening for all. After listening to each other's stories everyone felt better. The realization that they all sailed in the same boat, the boat of a stage of life where "heartbreak" was a normal occurrence made them relaxed about their vented feelings.

Arunima clapped, jumped and maintained the lead in smearing Ritwik's face with the birthday cake; then she scurried around the room and smudged other immaculate faces with the cake, deriving maximum fun. The enthusiasm and excitement at the party was contagious. The brief birthday session rekindled the dormant spirit of fun and helped the students blow away the cobwebs from their lives. The forthcoming semester exam seemed like a cakewalk now. She brought smiles back, not only on Ritwik's face, but also to all those who attended the party.

She became popular for her jovial temperament. She had a knack of bringing a smile on sullen faces and was informally anointed the birthday manager and given the title of "Queen of smiles".

FIVE

THE MID TERM was just over. There were no classes that day. Suman had planned a peaceful siesta. After lunch she came back to the room feeling a bit sleepy, and stretched out on her cot, folding her hands under her head on the pillow. She did not want Anu to disturb her so she didn't latch the door. But no sooner had Suman slipped into her beautiful land of dreams, she felt something digging into her armpit, and she opened her eyes with a shriek!

Arunima covered Suman's mouth with her hand and said, 'Stop! Stop! Are you planning to get all the hostel girls here?'

Suman rose from the bed looking terrified. She forcefully removed Arunima's hand from her mouth and said, 'Anu what is this? Stop troubling me! You know your pranks scare the hell out of me!'

But what Suman was saying had no impact on Arunima. She was very excited!

'Come on, Suman! Just forget everything. We are going to CG road today,' Anu said holding both of Suman's hands. She looked into her eyes making an earnest request.

Before Suman could try to understand the plan by asking further questions, Arunima added another line.

'Don't ask me why, what etc. etc, ok! Just get ready fast!'

Arunima was not listening to what Suman wanted to say. 'Hey buddy, can we leave this conversation for the transit time, while we are on the way to CG Road.'

Suman threw in the towel because it was a better option than convincing Arunima, or even trying to know exactly what was in her mind.

She got up from the bed thinking, "No sleep time in my destiny today." But then she looked at Arunima's face, exuding happiness that was rarely seen for her own self. She had been going out of her way to bring smiles to others, and it was the first time she was asking Suman to do something for her. And Suman thought that foregoing her sleep was not a big deal for that lovely smile on her dearest friend's face.

Arunima spread out half the clothes in her wardrobe on her bed, even some on Suman's. Finally, she picked up a peekaboo blood red mini dress. The dress looked beautiful. It clung to her body tightly and she looked very pretty with her thin waist and flat belly. Her fair skin shimmered through the deep scoop neck. The nude heels, swaying earrings and swanky sunglasses made her look stunning.

Suman widened her eyes, 'Wow babes, you can give competition to the best models walking the ramp. But hey, how will I manage the bloodshed of hearts you are going to cause today?'

Arunima laughed and said, 'Stop kidding! You can also try one.'

'Anu darling, I am happy in my denims.'

'And THE KURTA…' Arunima chimed in. 'Why are you such a bore?' asked Arunima, playfully. 'But, I hope my bore, but best friend wouldn't want me to get late!'

'Sure, I'm ready. But why don't you tell me where we are going?' Suman started losing her patience.

'Suman, just a few more minutes and you will know.'

Suman had no choice but to patiently follow her friend's lead. They walked a short distance and hailed a cab. Even during that miniscule walk, there was not a person whom they crossed who did not pause to ogle at Arunima. Suman felt awkward at all the lustful looks directed at Arunima but her friend actually seemed to thrive on the attention.

Her patience was finally rewarded when Arunima instructed the driver to stop the car before the famous swanky restaurant.

'Arunima, why have you brought me here? Why do you want to spend money unnecessarily?'

'Hey, don't worry; here we are guests of a very special person!' She chuckled.

Suman did not like this humour. 'Anu, enough, I don't know this person and you have made me an uninvited guest!'

Arunima was prepared for this kind of reaction from her. She said, 'As a friend, can I not make some choices on your behalf because I want your help in taking a decision. I have brought you to meet my boyfriend and know your opinion about him.'

Suman could not help smiling, 'Hey…Anu…you are such a *chhupa rustam*. All this while I had been thinking that you couldn't keep a thing to yourself alone, but it seems you have a whole other side to you. Why did you keep me in suspense? I mean, you call me your best friend!'

'Because, even I am not sure how serious he is about our relationship. I did not know what to tell you. Suman, in fact, I am just not aware when Avinash became interested in me. He called up this morning to tell me that he is in town after his business trip to Europe. And that he has come all the way, just to see me. I met him at a dance party, at a common friend's place. Thereafter, we met at a couple of parties, and kept in touch only through the phone like I do with my other friends. But, when he called me up today, and stated his feelings for me, I became confused. So, I need your help to assess how sincere his expressions are! May be, all alone, it will be difficult for me to assess his genuineness.'

'But, what about you Anu? Do you like him?' Suman asked.

Anu nodded happily.'Suman, my heartbeats quicken when I talk to him, which does not happen with anyone else. And I enjoy his company. Maybe I am in love! I cannot tell you how restless I have become after his call this morning.'

Suman smiled and said, 'So baby...you are in love!'

Arunima's countenance mirrored her emotions. She coyly dropped her eyelids while mentioning him with her lips stretching into a beautiful smile; her face turned pink and the glow of happiness made her look yet more beautiful. Suman had heard the word called love innumerable times, chanted all around her, but she was witnessing it for the first time on her dearest friend's face.

They entered the restaurant and occupied a table near the entrance.

A black Mercedes entered the restaurant's portico and a glamorous looking man descended from the car. As he walked towards the door, Arunima's beaming face made it clear this was Avinash.

And then Arunima said with great pride, 'Look Suman,

that is Avinash.' She waved at him as he walked in.

Avinash looked handsome! Like Arunima, he too appeared quite brand conscious; from top to bottom whatever he wore carried the mark of a brand. He was tall, fair and clean-shaven, with sharp features. The smart young man in charcoal trousers and a crisp white dress-shirt looked quite impressive. Arunima had already moved a few steps forward to greet him and display her affection. He walked with a swagger, like he owned the world. He hugged Arunima really tight and said, 'Hey! You look gorgeous!' Saying that he moved on to kiss her quite blatantly, not bothering about the attention they were attracting.

Suman felt awkward at Arunima and her boyfriend's overt display of affection. From the way Avinash behaved, no one could guess that their relationship was just as old as Arunima had told Suman.

Arunima must have whispered something in his ears and he diverted his attention to Suman. Arunima looked at her searchingly and Suman gave her a gentle nod and smile, conveying she had liked Avinash. Though she would never have approved of Avinash's public display of affection, but then Arunima was also an extrovert. Suman knew that for Arunima, his behaviour was quite normal.

Arunima then introduced her beau, 'Avi, meet my friend Suman. And Suman, this is Avinash Khetarpal.'

Avinash brought forward his hand for a handshake and said, 'Hi horny.'

Suman was aghast!

Arunima jumped in and corrected Avinash, 'He means HONEY.'

'Yeah, she is right,' said Avinash.

Suman had to reciprocate by shaking hands, as his hand was still extended for a handshake. Avinash held Suman's hand in a firm grip and tried to feel the skin of her palm with a slight rub which made Suman uncomfortable. There was no match between his appearance and his manners, Suman thought. His accent was rustic and his eyes wily. 'Arunima, your friend is as hot and spicy as you are,' Avinash was saying with a leer.

Suman was a bit miffed to hear this. 'Sir, we are not food that you can qualify us with tastes!'

'Aww,' he said, smiling forcefully. 'I was just joking! Your friend is very sensitive, darling,' he said, looking at Arunima and giggling foolishly.

Suman found him foul and uncouth, and her face showed her feelings. Arunima tried to cool her down, 'Come on Suman. Don't be so serious all the time.'

'Yeah!' Suman managed to get her composure back. Arunima's happy face made her forget Avinash's gaucherie.

Arunima giggled, wrapping her arm around his elbow

to form a loop. She pulled him along to look for a table of his choice. Suman followed them, all red in the face, but unable to decide what to do. She wanted to leave right away, but her concern for Arunima did not let her do so.

Avinash insisted on taking the seats towards the end of the room, away from the sight of the crowd in the restaurant. After comfortably occupying the corner seats, he said, 'Ok let's each of us also place our order.'

Suman was not at ease in his company. She pulled up all her courage and requested Arunima, 'Anu, is it alright if I leave now? Why don't you guys carry on? I have to leave early as I need to see the bookstore.' But Arunima wouldn't hear of it and insisted that she stay on, and Suman agreed. After ordering the drinks, Suman, though unwillingly, had to get involved in conversation with Avinash.

He had put one arm around Arunima's shoulders, and with his other hand he held her hand. His hand on Arunima's shoulder kept shifting to and fro and rested upon the skin near the cleft of her breasts. His eyes sparkled while doing this. He kept fiddling with her bare skin, and gradually pushed his fingers further towards her breasts.

Arunima removed his hand. 'Avinash, stop it!' She looked towards Suman silently apologizing for his actions.

Avinash immediately apologized, 'Sorry ladies! I didn't realize where my hand was. But ma'am,' looking at Suman he said, 'May I kiss my love? She is simply irresistible.'

Suman hung her head, and Anu said, 'Avi, please don't tease Suman. Suman, he is just trying to make you comfortable.'

What was this way of making someone feel comfortable, wondered Suman? But she kept quiet. The man's manners, in Suman's opinion were far away from being classified as those of a gentleman; they were actually crossing the line of decency. Suman's thoughts were becoming transparent on her face, and she almost stood up to leave the place.

'Suman we are very good friends, and Avinash cheers me up like this. He is quite spirited at times. You chill and relax!'

Arunima's ways had always appeared weird to Suman. She understood them to be the difference of expression acceptable in high society. So, the way the two of them were behaving could be a normal way of manifestation of their feelings for each other, Suman thought.

Arunima could make out Suman's uneasiness so she changed the topic of their discussion. 'Avi, what happened to your Europe contract?'

'Well, I never take no for an answer. Of course, I have signed the contract.' Avinash bragged a great deal about himself and the extent and expanse of his business empire.

For Suman, spending every minute was like years and she hurriedly gulped her drink and took leave of the couple.

Avinash's body language also made her feel guilty of playing gooseberry. She did not have a good opinion about him. But, it was a truth that Arunima was completely smitten by him.

Should she discourage Arunima from getting into a relationship with the man? Would she listen to her? May be her thoughts were outdated as per current society, or maybe she belonged to a class different from Arunima, and they followed different social norms. Was she wrong in her thoughts because she believed that physical proximity between a man and a woman demanded some limits of decency, or was she being too conservative in her ideas and opinion of the modern world.

Probably Arunima was the modern woman, and she represented the changing face of today's society. It was difficult for Suman to decide whether to state her opinion about Avinash to her, or to simply support her decision because Avinash made her friend happy.

SIX

ARUNIMA GOT BACK to the hostel just before the gates closed, looking thrilled to bits.

She came and sat next to Suman and said, 'Suman I can't tell you how happy I am!'

'That I know without you telling me.'

'Ok, then you must guess the reason too.'

'Oh, come on! The reason is as obvious as an elephant in a room.'

'Avinash, yes! But what in particular?'

'You spent your entire day with your love, what else could it be?'

'Suman, can you even imagine the things we did?'

'How can I know?'

'Just guess!'

'Well, you must have gone for a movie, and for sure you had dinner with him! Which movie did you watch?' Suman asked.

'Oh Suman, your imagination cannot go beyond a set norm. Silly girl, I was in bed with Avinash, and we made love, and more love! I cannot begin to describe how wonderful it all was.' Arunima still looked as if she were in a trance. She picked up a pillow and embraced it tightly, as if it were Avinash.

What Arunima stated as moment of fun appeared as a catastrophe to Suman.

'Suman, all the doubts I had about Avi's intentions have become clear. I thank my stars for giving me a person like him in my life. A caring, generous and loving partner; what more could I have asked for?' Arunima was on her flight of fancy with Avinash, and she seemed to be in a palace where happiness and love existed without any bounds.

Suman's eyes were opened to a harsh reality. People's value systems could be very different from hers. What was an absolute sin in her eyes could be just a random activity for another. In Arunima's world, men and women clearly had the same parameters of enjoyment. If men could indulge in casual intimacy, so could women. Suman's thought process was changing too; she was learning to accept as a reality what she saw happen around her. "Sex" did not appear a term of taboo as it had been before she befriended Arunima. Arunima would talk about condoms as if she were talking about candies!

Suman had her perception changing about the world. She was witnessing a metamorphosis of the value system; the iconoclasm of existing social norms. But, weren't the older systems offering greater emotional and mental protection—a better cushion against getting exposed to human vagaries? Is breaking rules exposing us to greater vulnerability and leading us to initial stage of civilization from where we started our journey towards development?

There was a conundrum that had emerged before Suman, with no apparent solution.

SEVEN

THE COURSE FOR the final batch was nearing its end, and it was the best time to relive the memories, both good and bad, of the days spent at the institute. To find student groups straining their minds and exchanging their special memories, and marveling at the mettle of surviving through the two years of rigorous schedule, was a common scene at the institute.

Prateek, Pranjal, and Suman were sipping coffee together in the canteen while Satwik sat alone at an adjacent table. A moment later, he too joined them by pulling his chair near theirs, and as usual started with his mimicry of their various professors. Gradually, other students also joined in the guffaws. The ripples of uncontrollable laughter set many a belly aching. Surprisingly, Arunima, who always led such shows was conspicuous by her absence. Everyone wondered where she could be and, obviously, looked to Suman for an answer. Suman too was wondering as she got up from her seat, 'Where could she be? After her no dues certificate, she was supposed to join me here in the canteen.'

Without any delay, she left the group to look for her. She was trying to recollect whether Arunima had shared some information that she was missing out, or maybe she had told her something that she had not heard. She just drew a complete blank.

Suman checked all of Arunima's favourite hangouts in the campus; the TV room, the sports complex, she was nowhere! No one could provide any clues about her. All through Suman's stay at the institute, it was the first time she had to be on the look-out for Arunima. At all other times, it would always be Arunima who complained that Suman was missing, and to be able to locate her was a great achievement. Suman started getting worried now. Maybe Avinash was in town and Arunima might have gone to meet him... With this thought, Suman moved to her room to get her mobile, which she had forgotten to carry with her.

As she opened the door, the reek of tobacco smoke filled her nostrils. The smoke had risen till the end of the roof. A few white smoke rings were still travelling up almost about to merge their identity with the white, smoky room air. Under Arunima's bed was an ashtray filled with cigarette stubs, a half cigarette still burning over the tray. She was lying in bed, her face digging in the pillow. And it was apparent what Arunima had been doing the whole day; but why?

She had stayed in her room the whole day without food; cigarettes providing the day's subsistence. Arunima had quit smoking long back, then why was she smoking now?

'Anu,' Suman called out while still near the door.

'What has happened, Anu? Are you all right?' Suman forced Arunima to raise her face from the pillow.

'Anu, what happened?' Suman asked again.

Arunima's eyes were swollen; her face red and her pillow sodden.

'Oh, I am fine!' Arunima sat up and spoke, trying to look normal, but her condition spoke louder than her words.

'Anu! You are hiding something from me, come on, look at my face, and tell me what's the matter?' Suman said raising Arunima's chin with her hand.

Arunima clasped Suman tightly and broke down. 'Suman, tell me how it feels when your world of dreams is razed by someone, and that 'someone' is none other than the one with whom you dreamt about the beautiful world!'

'Anu, you are talking in riddles. Tell me what has happened?'

Arunima blabbered it all out while still clinging to her, 'Suman I was wrong about Avinash; he is a big cheat; he has ditched me!' She sobbed with great pain, tears streaming down her face.

Suman shook Arunima, 'Anu, can you please tell me what Avinash has done that you are upset to this extent. I have never seen you so shattered before!'

Arunima, with great effort, controlled her tears. She said, 'Suman I am pregnant. I called him up right away to share the news. And the moment I disclosed to him that I was pregnant with his child, he shouted at me on the phone. He wants me to get rid of this child or else he will wash his hands off me. In fact he has already done so. He stopped taking my calls. Today he texted me that he is leaving this country with his fiancée.'

'What!' Suman shouted. 'Pregnant…when did you come to know about it?'

'About a week ago. I thought I would share this news with you after convincing Avinash that at least we get engaged. And I was damn sure he would agree to it, because I had seen him so passionate whenever I met him.'

'Oh my god!' Suman was shocked.

She felt quite helpless, as there was not much she could do for Arunima. Maybe she held herself to be partly responsible for Arunima's condition. Had she stopped her by being candid about Avinash, she might have prevented her from getting into this mess.

Suman had an inkling of Avinash being a cheat, right at the time she had met him, but she had not shared her opinion with Arunima thinking that it might hurt her. Suman was cursing herself for her timidity. Her action, then, was supported by good intention, but calling a spade a spade is better than playing to the gallery as it can have repercussions more serious than one can think of. It was true that Suman wanted Arunima to be happy and so she wished to be wrong in her opinion of Avinash. But she was not able to exonerate herself from the remorse of being responsible for Arunima's plight. Suman could not do anything other than consoling her and providing her moral support.

Arunima was shouting and tearing the pillow in her hands, as if she would have killed Avinash had he been there in front of her.

Stories of women getting into bed with men without any commitment are becoming rather commonplace, thought Suman. Maybe women consider this a step towards their empowerment. Some also have a reason for it—enhancement of career, or for ending the frustration of a broken relationship, but when it comes to lovemaking with feelings from the heart involved, the case is different.

Such a relationship remains a source of joy forever; such an experience nourishes the soul all through life.

Whether a boon or a curse, the fact remains that nature has created the physiology of a woman for child bearing. Her biological composition puts on her a greater onus of creating an entity in this world. A man has an option to slip away from the responsibility, but a woman can't!

Suman tried to placate Arunima, 'Anu you have been deceived—true, and the fact remains that you alone have to bear the brunt. But don't think yourself to be alone, I am always there for you.Time might heal your wounds, and painful memories but what about the new life thriving within you? Anu, I think you should get an abortion done. You cannot spoil your entire life because of someone else's folly.'

Arunima had cried all her tears it seemed, and no more tears came forth. She listened to Suman silently, with no expression on her face. Then suddenly, her face and body changed to look decisive. She wiped the tears, which had already dried, and inhaled deeply. She said, 'Suman, it could be a momentary satisfaction of his senses for Avinash, but for me it was the moment of love that I cherished. I am ready to be responsible for this act of mine, which is priceless for me. I will give birth to my child. It will be a symbol of my genuine love.'

Suman hugged Arunima to lend support for her decision. Having done that, she thought of something and said, 'But Anu, how will you handle your condition all alone? Why don't you join me till the time you have your baby? My family and I will see you through it all. And it is hardly a matter of a few months.'

Arunima hugged her. 'Suman, mere thanks wouldn't do justice to the feelings I have for you.In the past two years while I stayed at the institute, a lot has happened on my family front, which I could not share with you because I only thought about Avinash all this while. Dad had another lady in his life, whom he married secretly, and when Mom came to know about this she left Dad and came to stay with her father. Of her two siblings, mom's elder brother and his family stayed with Grandpa and looked after the family business. Her younger brother is working at a senior position in a refinery at Vadodara.He lives with his wife as they do not have kids.

Only after a few months, Grandpa passed away and Mom's elder brother grabbed hold of all the property. Mom had just a piece of land in her name, which Grandpa had given her at the time of marriage. She sold off a part of it, and established her garment export unit in the remaining land. Since then, she has left Grandpa's house, and stays alone in a rented accommodation. Mom counts on her younger brother for support. Mom's elder brother did not give anything to his younger brother either; he claimed all the property as his because he was managing the business. He has breached the trust of his siblings. But let it be. It's Mom's family and she knows best about her family affairs. And Mamu—that is how I address my younger uncle, is quite content with whatever he has. His adorable wife is from Dubai, but she follows Indian traditions better than an Indian.

So, I have decided to be with Mom, and we both will be available for each other. Mom will support my decision. She feels quite guilty now that she neglected me for the sake of enjoying her life. The sweetness of a mother-daughter relationship we missed earlier—we shall be making amends for it from now on. As for my baby, I hope I shall be able to convince her on that. After all, she is my Mom.' And a relaxed smile appeared on Arunima's face. Both Arunima and Suman felt calm after the decision.

EIGHT

'RAJAN, NOW YOU know the whole story. My crazed actions were all due to that swindler. I have witnessed Anu in trauma because of that wicked person. And I cannot let this person repeat his shabby game with Saloni.'

Rajan had remained alert and thoughtful all this while. 'Suman, why don't you call up your cousin to tell her about Avinash,' he suggested.

Then, just as Suman picked up her cell phone, a thought struck him, and he suggested, 'I think talking about such a grave issue should be done face to face. For now, Suman, you call her up, and subtly warn her against the man. Then plan a meeting where you can explain what you want to by telling her the entire story that you narrated to me. I'm sure being your cousin, she would be wise enough to save herself from that man's trap!'

'I just hope Saloni listens to me...'Suman muttered as she dialled her.

The call was answered. Before Suman could ask her a question, Saloni said in an excited tone, 'Suman, what a great coincidence; I was thinking of talking to you to share the news that I have entered the semi-final round of the musical challenge of a TV channel. The company which is sponsoring the event is paying for our trip to Mumbai and I am going with Mom tomcrrow morning to Mumbai.'

'Congratulations, my dear! When will you be back?'

'Well, if I qualify the semi-final round then I will be back only after two weeks, but if not, then may be in four to five days.It depends on my performance in the semi-finals, you know!'

'Oh! You can't imagine how happy and relieved I am!'

'Happy, I understand, but relieved, why? Were you aware of my participation? Did Mom speak to you about this earlier?'

'Saloni, I think you need to do your packing so we will do all the talking when you are back from Mumbai. Wish you all the luck to win the final round and come back with the award. I am sure you will do it.'

'Thanks Suman, love you!' and the talk ended.

After talking to Saloni, Suman looked relaxed. 'As long

as she is with Kavita Masi, I don't need to worry about her,' she murmured.

'Suman, it's good that Saloni will be away with her mother, for both you and her. The sleepless nights you were going to have due to Saloni would have affected your work, and you know very well that we cannot afford to get lax at this juncture. The international project, which is our responsibility, demands our complete attention.'

'Thanks, Rajan. Thanks for being with me,' Suman said, grateful for his presence through her turmoil.

'I am with you Suman, always.' Both kept holding hands and looking into each other's eyes. Their eyes remained locked, trying to communicate the feelings in their hearts.

The exhaustion due to the entire day's running around had put Suman low on physical energy, but she was charged emotionally. Rajan acted as a great emotional soother, and to be with a person who could understand and care, was nothing less than bliss! Next day was Sunday—the family day—a day when everyone got the opportunity to unwind by spending time in family gossip or eating out or doing things which suited them.The beginning of relaxation started from Saturday night. Suman looked forward to weekends to spend time with her hamily.

She came out into the hall wearing her night suit—the striped pajamas and a round necked T-shirt with her hair flowing loose and reaching till her waist. She walked into the living room, tying her hair into a knot at the nape of her neck. Stretching, she looked around, taking in the family. Dad and Mom were busy in their work and her siblings seemed to be still in their rooms. Newspapers were littered all around the living room, on the centre table, sofa, and the dining table.

"It had to be the work of her brother, who would have ransacked the newspaper to cut pictures of his favourite sports news and the players," she thought. She moved from one spot to another, picking up odds and ends, tidying up the room.

She noticed the newspapers were all intact, and only the matrimonial pages carried red markings at random places.

"Heavens, what's all this!" And it hardly took any time for her to understand that the effort was to look for a suitable groom for her. It was the work of her parents who scanned the entire matrimonial pages with a fine toothcomb, and underlined the ads that they considered suitable for her—the basis being the qualification and family background of the groom

Suman did not feel upset this time, as she used to do earlier, whenever she overheard her parents discuss marriage proposals for her.

And she made up her mind to introduce Rajan to her parents, and express her desire and her choice to make him her life partner.

"But I think we will have to wait till the guests depart from India after endorsing the basic formalities of the project," Suman said to herself, "I am sure Mom and Dad will be happy to meet him." She blushed thinking of Rajan as her groom. Till a few days back she had no such feelings for Rajan, and now not a minute went without him being a part of her thoughts. How does an acquaintance become the most important person in one's life? Suman could not understand.

She went back to the time when she had first joined this company and met Rajan.

NINE

SUMAN HIRED A cab for her first day to office. Dressed in a white chikan kurta, navy blue jeans and an embroidered muslin scarf matching the colour of her jeans.

'Mom, please hurry up! I need to be in time, I don't want to be late on my first day at work,' said Suman, rushing through a last minute check of her folder that held her appointment letter and other important documents. She and her two friends had got placement in Maryland Inc., which had recruited them at the highest package of the year.

Savita tried to hurriedly assemble puja things in a plate. She wouldn't let her daughter move out to begin the first day of her career without following all the rituals; the rituals would guarantee an auspicious start, she believed! She applied a small red dot of vermillion on Suman's forehead and fed her a spoon of sweet curd.

'Please Mamma!' Suman pleaded affectionately as she took Savita's hand and placed it over her head, seeking her blessings and said, 'just wish me good luck from your heart and all evils coming my way will be gone!'

Suman never found those rituals of any significance, but she valued the concern and love behind them. She believed that a mother's prayers had the power to protect her children.

Savita, like an understanding mother, allowed her daughter to move out, but she could not help her eyes tearing up. She was proud of her daughter's achievements.

Suman's cab headed for office at a rather slow speed because of the terrible traffic on the road; the traffic lights added to her woes, taking ages to turn from red to green. There were long serpentine queues of vehicles waiting at traffic signals. Suman had kept enough time margin for such unavoidable delays.

She looked at her wristwatch to check the time, and took heart seeing she had plenty of time before her reporting hour. The rest of the road seemed clear of traffic. So, in another ten minutes she could comfortably manage to reach office. She took out her mobile to call her other friends to know where they were. They all planned to report together, and in case anyone reached early, they would wait for the others!

But before she could get her call connected, there was

a strong jerk; the cab halted. Suman got her attention back to the road in front of her. There was no traffic signal, no traffic jam either, then why did the cab stop? Before Suman could ask anything, the driver got off the cab and opened its bonnet to check for the problem. Suman was getting restless inside the vehicle so she too came out.

She went closer to the driver making an effort to detect the fault in the engine, and peeped inside as if she would unearth the defect and get the cab going. But, alas! her knowledge of engines was as poor as her knowledge of French and Latin! The best she could do was to ask rather sternly, 'Are you hurrying up, or do I look for some other cab?'

The driver looking worked up said, 'Madam this cab cannot move any further. There seems to be a major problem in the engine. I am so sorry, I think you need to take another cab.'

This was terrible news. Suman had not expected such an answer from the driver, even though for valid reasons. She instantly realized her mistake and making amends for her rude speech said in a soft tone, 'Please, at least arrange for another cab, or else I will be late to work.'

The driver responded and tried to stop vehicles by giving them signals to stop. But, it was the peak office hour, and everyone seemed to be in a race to accomplish his or her mission of reaching office in time.

She dared not enter the overcrowded DTC bus so what was left for her to do? To wait! But for what! Yes, to exercise the last option and that was to hitch a ride.

Though hitching a ride with a stranger was defying her parents' strict instructions for playing safe in Delhi, but it was the only option left! She and her friends had been thumbing rides many times during their college days, but they did so together, in a group.

Cursing, praying and then begging—it was all going on!

'Oh god, I was telling Mom that all these rituals are useless. God please, help me! How will I reach my office?'

She looked at her watch again; it was beyond the reporting time mentioned in the joining letter, and hopelessness was replacing her euphoria.

She was still making up her mind whether to go to office or go back home with an excuse for not being able to join on that day. With an indecisive mind she walked a few steps and there she could see a white car approaching from the road in front of her, going towards the direction she had to go. She pointed her thumb towards the direction she had to go, and the car came to a halt.

'Can you please drop me at the spot nearest to Connaught Place?' asked Suman. The stranger opened the car door to let her in. There was only one seat occupied, and that was the driver's seat. With some apprehension, she took her place next to the driver and closed the door. She tried to look at the face of the person from the corner of her eye because he did not seem to be in a mood to talk, or maybe he was dumb and could not talk! Well, she could not take the risk of breaking the ice; she maintained silence and concentrated on the way ahead, so as not to miss the spot to get down.

As they entered the outer ring of CP, he asked, 'Where do you have to get down?'

Suman did not want to extend her welcome so she thought of disembarking then and there itself. She nodded, 'Yeah, this is fine!' At least he can speak, she thought and smiled.

He parked the car near a pedestrian path, where she could descend with ease.

Suman unlocked the door and said, 'Thanks a lot, sir.'

'Not at all,' he said!

She turned to look at his face. His lips were tight like those of a robot, and Suman's desire to smile at him remained locked in her.

'Ah...h! What an appalling beginning of my first day!' she thought. 'I don't know what all I might have to face ahead in the day.'

Her office was still two kilometres away, and she hired an auto to reach there. After all the drama, she landed half an hour later than the scheduled reporting time. Her friends had already showed up and completed the signing in formalities.

It was an embarrassment! She should have gone back and reported on the next day, but that could have led to, maybe, graver consequences, she thought. Avoiding questioning glances, she followed the HR manager with her head bent. But, there are a few souls on this earth who miss no chance to make digs at people in distress.

'Hi! A newcomer?' A slimy voice asked the manager.

Suman lifted her head to look at the person. A lady in her middle age; her shoulder length straightened hair was dyed a strong mahogany and a big black bindi adorned her forehead. She looked ravishing in her black chiffon sari with golden border and almost backless blouse—certainly inappropriate office dressing and to Suman she appeared to be the quintessential office vamp. 'The new generation is quite confident. People from my generation cannot afford to be late even after 15 years of service. Anyway, all the best!' The lady spoke with barely disguised malice.

The HR manager, Mr Shukla, was quite understanding and sympathetic. He carried enough wealth of silver on his head, which surely had a connection with his professional wisdom. He tried to console her, 'Just keep your cool; don't get bothered by such comments.'

Suman nodded her head to acknowledge what

Mr Shukla said and took a deep calming breath!

She mutely followed him, well prepared to bear the consequences of being late, even though it was just a delay of half an hour! Not quite unusual for a place like Delhi, where traffic jams are quite frequent. She walked behind him, making him a shield to get protection from any other bad experience.

Mr Shukla led her to a room, and as she stepped in, she observed that it was quite different from the rest of the office area; the fragrance of fresh flowers and the room freshener invigorated her dying spirits. The room looked tidier than the rest of the office. She could see her reflection in the marble floor shining below her feet. The files were neatly stacked on a stool next to the cushioned executive chair. A vase containing fresh white and pink chrysanthemums was placed on a glass-topped table. At a glance she could scan the entire room. But, she could not see any person in the room. Mr Shukla gestured her to sit on the chair, and he too occupied a chair facing the executive chair on the other side of the table.

Mr Shukla told her,'You are lucky to have Mr Mathur as your boss.'

Before she mustered courage to ask a question about Mr Mathur, a voice called out from the back, 'Mr Shukla, how are you doing?'

Both of them turned to look at the person speaking and Suman responded by almost jumping out of her chair, as if she had stepped on a snake. Undeterred by Suman's reaction, he walked in with long steps to occupy his executive chair, and began the conversation. 'Tell me, Mr Shukla, what brings you here? Who is this young lady? Have we met earlier?' looking at Suman he asked.

Mr Shukla, without wasting any time, spoke up, 'Sir, Ms Suman is joining us as a management trainee from today, and she will be reporting to you.'

Mr Shukla left after the formal introduction. Suman was wondering—was he really not able to recognize her, or was he pretending because of arrogance? She did not like him for his indifference. Confused, she looked at him.

The boss was looking at the papers that Mr Shukla had handed to him, which also comprised of Suman's bio data. And he seemed to recover his lost memory, 'Are you the one who came with me to CP in my car?'

Suman nodded her head.

'Yeah…got it!' he said, exulting. It appeared as if he had regained some lost treasure! Suman's lips curled up into smile. At least he had recovered from the bout of amnesia, otherwise she would have to repeat the explanation for being late.

He apologized to Suman, 'I'm so sorry; I did not

recognize you right away; I was preoccupied.'

'It's ok! It can happen with anyone.' And Suman's smile extending to her entire face reassured him that she did not feel bad.

The boss, Mr Mathur, as he was being addressed, flipped through the pages of her documents folder, while Suman fiddled with her ball point pen nervously. The first day at office with no known faces around was like being in a land of aliens. She was not aware of behavioral protocol in an office environment. So, she waited for her boss to cut the first turf.

And finally, Suman's patience bore fruit. The boss was praising her credentials.

'You have an excellent academic record, Ms Suman.' He started to look at her folder from the first page, again. With every page he turned, he had an adjective to admire her performance, and it bolstered Suman's confidence.

Suman felt quite at ease now.

'Thanks, Sir!' she said.

'Well, I hope you won't mind if I address you as Suman and wish that you too call me by my first name, Rajan.'

'Yes, Ok!' Suman said with a grin.

She admired this gesture. She was quite sure that it would be a pleasure working with a person like Rajan!

Very soon, she knew that Rajan did not only have good EQ, but he also possessed excellent IQ.

He practically explained the organizational theories which she had learned at the institute through his slide presentation. After going through the presentation, she understood the outline of the organization structure, which might have taken her months to understand otherwise!

She was getting bewitched. As the interaction progressed, she felt drawn towards the aura of charm around him, a strange sort of magnetism. His thin lips forming into shapes to deliver something similar to a college lecture, and the fisted right hand with upright forefinger coordinated its movement on the computer screen with the words he spoke. With his left hand, he pressed the keys on the keyboard to shift the slides. For Suman, the words echoed into strange sounds, as her eyes got stuck in his almond shaped dark brown eyes. Her heart swelled with a strong current of emotion to sweep her away into a world of dreams, where she wanted to admit to him that he was the first person in her life whom she had started liking, for no reason at all!

His only concern was his work, and that was to help a trainee employee learn about the organization. He seemed bothered about the tasks remaining to be done, and there was no sign of getting admiration from the opposite sex to boost his ego. His indifference became a trap for Suman.

Someone whispered to her, "He is your Mr perfect." And she awoke to her own heart's proclamation.

Rajan got up from his chair, opened the cupboard and pulled out booklets with glossy papers.

Suman got some more time to analyze her boss, and a question rocked her mind, "Was he good enough to look at?"

Though Suman considered beauty as only skin deep. In this case, she had fallen head over heels for Rajan—attractive or not attractive was not important. He was her Mr Perfect! So what if he was not tall or handsome like a typical Mills and Boon hero? But her heart declared that he was her hero.

Rajan brought a large number of information bulletins with some loose papers, and passed them to Suman, who was still lost in the fight between her heart and mind. Instead of placing them on the table after accepting them, she dropped them on the floor.

Rajan, caught unawares, looked at Suman, who had instantly bent down to grab hold of the papers which lay scattered in the room, and some loose ones started sliding slowly out of the room, through the slit beneath the door. Rajan joined Suman in her effort to gather the booklets and sheets. Both of them sprinted to grab hold of the page that made its way out of the room and Suman's left hand was caught in the tight clasp of Rajan's right hand. It also led to Rajan's left hand resting on Suman's boobs, as her back was checked by the wall behind her.

It was an embarrassing state and a strange one too!

Suman could feel the tough muscles of Rajan's arm, and Rajan felt the softness of Suman's breasts as his hand momentarily rested on her vigorously throbbing chest. Their hands remained firmly together in a bid to prevent the other from falling. Suman slid on the floor and Rajan maintained his balance and stood up. For the few moments that their hands remained together, Suman felt her body melting in his tough masculine clasp, and she seemed to lose all her strength.

Rajan bent down to a level where he could see directly into Suman's eyes. He offered his other hand to her and helped her stand up. Suman got the support of his hand, and had to clutch his shoulders with her other hand to get the strength back in her legs.

Both stood dusting themselves and straightening rumpled clothes to look tidy again. Those few seconds got eternalized in Suman's mind as one of the most beautiful moments. As a matter of courtesy, she apologized. 'I'm so sorry! How could I create such a mess!' and she pretended to look disgusted.

Rajan recovered and tried to look comfortable saying, 'It's alright, don't worry about it.' And then he came back to his chair.

'I think we can get back to work after a cup of coffee.' He picked up his intercom receiver and checked with Suman,

'What would you prefer—tea or coffee?'

'Coffee would be great.'

Both sipped their coffee with Suman's head sunk low over the papers in her hand, and Rajan's eyes glued to the computer screen.

'Suman, till the time you have a place allotted, you might have to sit in my room. I hope you are ok with it?'

'Yes, absolutely fine!' she said without any expression, but thought she could not have been granted anything better!

Rajan read Suman's serious face to convey she was not happy with this and said, 'If you want you can sit in the conference room, but you might have to move out whenever someone comes for a meeting.'

'But for me this place is absolutely okay,' Suman said with a smile this time.

Rajan nodded with his lips stretching into a sexy smile. Suman's heart skipped a beat, and her eyes got fixed on Rajan again. Before she ended up making another blunder, she regained her composure and tried to concentrate on the papers in her hand.

But, her mind did not coordinate with her eyes, and it waded through feelings tingling in her heart. The peon entered the room carrying a tray with food served in two plates. He arranged the plates and the cutlery on the table kept in the corner of the room with two cushioned chairs.

'What's this?' asked Suman.

'What can you expect during lunch time?' asked Rajan.

'But...but, how come he is getting food in two plates?'

'Because, I asked him to get food for both of us from the canteen.'

'When?'

'When I ordered for coffee, right in front of your eyes!'

Suman felt embarrassed once again. She was so engrossed in her new experience that she had failed to notice what was going on!

'From my experience, I know that no one brings food on their first day at office,' Rajan said, making himself comfortable in the chair near the table where the food was kept. 'And if I am wrong, then let me have the pleasure of sharing your home cooked food.' He gestured Suman to join him to have food. Suman was dumbfounded, because she was really not carrying her food. She quite enjoyed playing the losing game with Rajan. He seemed to be a very understanding and caring person.

TEN

SUMAN LOOKED AROUND the cubicle; it was her new place in the office. It was not that she wanted a separate cabin, but she was missing Rajan. She was now one month old in the office, but for that one month she shared Rajan's cabin, each day was etched in her memory.

She became used to his appreciative glance. He looked at her and always noticed what was new in her dressing, or her hairstyle. He even suggested hairstyles that suited her long and silky hair. 'Suman, open hair suits your face, but even when you tie a knot with your silver pin tucked in it, you look gorgeous.' And from that day onwards, Suman kept her hair open, or made a knot at the nape of her neck.

'Suman you look pretty in pink; it matches the hue of your pink cheeks.' These words from Rajan tingled her and turned her cheeks to crimson from pink.

Whenever she noticed Rajan's gaze fixed on her, she felt flattered! And when he said, 'Suman you are so different from the other girls—so natural and simple, but still you could win a beauty contest from amongst the best dressed women.' Suman could not decide whether he was flirting or indeed these were his words of admiration for her! Whatever it was, she enjoyed it!

A new place, with a new assignment—how boring, thought Suman. To top it all, she felt quite low in spirits, may be due to being away from Rajan. But, she had to start working on the project to meet her deadline. She called up the office store to send her the stationery, and ordered for a cup of coffee in the canteen. She picked up the intercom to call up Rajan, and let him know that she wanted to join him for coffee.But she desisted! What if Rajan said no? Maybe he wouldn't want to be bothered with her company now that it wasn't an absolute necessity.

She unwillingly inserted a CD containing the data to work on in the drive of her PC kept in the middle of the L shaped desk and waited for the screen to appear. A voice calling from behind her made her turn around with a jerk.

'Ma'am, Rajan sir wants to see you in his room.'

It was the canteen boy. 'What happened to my coffee?' asked Suman.

'Sir has asked to get your coffee also to his room.'

Feeling overjoyed, but not wanting Rajan to notice her restlessness, she moved to his room carrying a slip pad and a pen, as if she was being called to discuss something important.

Rajan waited with two cups of coffee on his table. Suman could see the eagerness on his face as she entered the room.

'Hi Suman! so all set at your new place.'

'Yes, sort of.'

'Good.'

'Any problem, just let me know,' he said with his head bent low to sip the coffee, and his eyes looking up towards her.

She shook her head and smiled gently.

'Suman, can I get a bit personal with you? I hope you would not mind that!'

'Not at all.'

'I believe that we should include some fun as part of our work; in fact, it can be a great recipe for improving efficiency at work. What do you say?'

'Absolutely,' Suman responded.

'So, how about having lunch outside?'

'Today?'

'Any problems?'

'No, no problem.' Though she wanted to take a rain

check on the offer, but she could not; an invitation to be with Rajan, and she saying no to it—no way!

'Ok done! I am reserving a table for both of us in a nearby restaurant. Believe me, you will love the food,' Rajan said with a sparkle in his eyes.

The restaurant was just a five-minute drive from office, so they had ample time for lunch.

The food was really good, and Suman loved it.

Rajan said, 'Suman this is my favourite hangout place!'

'Do you like it for any specific reason, or just like that?' Suman asked.

Rajan looked sad.

'Rajan, what happened?'

He spoke in a soft voice, 'I have lots of memories attached to this place, especially those of my childhood. I used to come here with my family quite often.'

'I could sense from your sad face that something made you nostalgic here! But the food is really a treat for the taste buds!'

'Who all are there in your family?'

'Only a brother settled abroad with his family.'

'And your parents?' Suman could sense something wrong.

'My parents are no more in this world. They both died in a plane crash a few months ago.'

'Oh! I am so sorry, Rajan.'

And Suman noticed a film of tears appearing in his eyes, which he tried to hide by blinking excessively.

Suman felt bad as if the mishap had a connection with her life, and grief choked her voice. She could not say a few words of solace to him.

Rajan continued to speak, 'I wish I could have met you earlier and introduced you to my parents whose greatest concern was to see me happily married.'

Suman was taken aback!

And, before her mind could register that Rajan was proposing, she dropped her spoon, and in a bid to pick that up from the floor, she bent down and hit the mocktail glass, which fell on the table and the drink spilled down on her lap.She was drenched in the liquid.

'Oh shit!' said Suman and ran towards the washroom.

Since that day, both Suman and Rajan didn't broach the subject.

At least, she became certain about Rajan's mind. The ball was in her court now! Suman was looking for an opportune moment to introduce Rajan to her parents.

ELEVEN

SUMAN HAD HER eyes shifting between the computer screen and the papers spread on her table. Pencils, pens and markers changed between the hold of her fingers, and she wished to finish the proofreading till the end of the draft report. The entire team had been working overtime for the past few days.

A special team of five executives was cherry picked by the top management with Rajan being their team leader. The team worked relentlessly, because the project with international collaboration not only meant a great leap for the company, but also perks for the special team. Rajan chose Suman to assist him, even though she was new in the company.

Suman finished the basic draft of the report and

decided to discuss it with Rajan before printing its final copy. She also wanted to invite him for lunch on the coming Sunday and introduce him to her family. Only after she introduced him, she could convince her parents about getting married to him.

She lifted her head to look at the wall clock.'Oh my god! It's 3 o'clock.'She didn't realize how the small arm of the clock had moved more than 120 degrees. Suman looked around, and the faces of the office staff grinned like that of a Cheshire cat. The employees were back after a treat to their palates in the office canteen or a heartening meal of their home made tiffins along with their gossip sessions.

She could now feel hunger making her intestines ache, and pulled out her drawer to have something to eat. She did not carry her tiffin that day, as she left home quite early; she preferred to order something from the canteen rather than trouble her mother. There was a packet of cookies, and she devoured four-five of them in seconds.

She closed the files, slid them in the drawer, switched off the computer, and then stood up to go to Rajan's room and order lunch. Having walked just a few steps, she saw Saloni in the office.

"Saloni! How come you are here?" Suman asked with an expression of disbelief.

Saloni responded with, 'Madam has become a VIP these days, so there was no other way to catch up with you. I checked up with Savita Masi and she said that it was difficult to find you at home these days.'

Suman ,with a forced smile, asked Saloni to follow her to her seat. She pulled an empty chair from the adjoining cubicle and asked her to sit.

'Saloni, I am extremely busy these days. But tell me, what emergency has brought you to my office?'

Saloni's thoughtful face made Suman worried. Avinash's face flashed before her eyes, and she recollected all the related events.

'Saloni, is everything fine?'

Suman prayed in her heart that Saloni should not share what was her greatest apprehension about Avinash. The fear scalded Suman's mind like molten lava.

Saloni began talking.'Suman please don't be amazed at the revelation I am about to make.'

'I know it has to do with the man with whom you are moving around, but I don't want to jump the gun regarding conclusions, so just tell me, in brief, that you have not damaged your life beyond repair.'

'No Suman! But, it is the truth that I collected all ingredients for a recipe of disaster that would have ruined my life.'

Suman exhaled and leaned back in the chair as the clutch of fear gripping her heart loosened.

'I met a guy named Avinash in a shopping mall. And it was all so weird, the situation in which I met him and we became friends and a relationship began to develop.'

'What!' asked Suman.

'He helped me pay my shopping bills because I was pickpocketed of all my cash and even the credit cards. And then, he also saved me from other unnecessary trouble, by calling my banks and registering complaints for my lost cards. In return, he insisted for a cup of coffee with me. And thereafter, he waited for me at the college gate and invited me for lunch I was totally bewitched by his charm. He took me out for lunch to posh restaurants. After moving around with him for a few days, I felt quite comfortable in his company.

'When he could sense that I was under his influence, he invited me to a night party with friends. But fortunately, I didn't join him because I had to go to Mumbai for my music competition. And now I realize that I have had such a narrow escape from all that could have happened!'Saloni uttered all this in one breath, and her face seemed to lose all colour to make her look pale and sickly

Suman's face tensed too. 'But why do you look so terrified?' she asked Saloni. 'Come on Saloni, tell me fast! What happened?'

And Saloni, rather than saying anything, took out a copy of the newspaper from her purse and spread it in front of Suman. Under the caption 'KINGPIN OF FLESH TRADE NABBED' was Avinash's handcuffed photo with a few more men and a lady. The story read:

"Police arrested a group of four persons for running a prostitution racket from a five-star hotel on Friday night at New Delhi. Avinash Khetrapal, 31, the main culprit, lures women with his riches and invites international clients by charging hefty sums from them."

'Saloni, you escaped by the skin of your teeth!' Suman felt her head swirling. She held her forehead with both her hands and rested her elbows on the table for support.

After stabilizing she said, 'Saloni, I was worried about you since I saw you with him. But he would turn out to be such a bastard was beyond even my wildest imagination. Anyway he is being taken care of in a manner he deserved, but why do you look worried when he is already under police custody?'

Saloni said, 'Suman, I am not worried about him stupid, I am worried about myself. I got a call from the police station that they want to see me tomorrow, or else they will come to my residence. And you know very well that if men or women in uniform visit my home, it will open a Pandora's Box of questions and problems for me?'

'Didn't you ask them, why?'

'Yeah, I did. The lady who had called said that my name figured in the list of persons he called frequently and also received calls from. So, they are interrogating all the persons with whom he had any kind of link.'

Suman looked thoughtful.

Saloni was saying,'Suman, from the time I have received the call, I am on pins and needles. I can't dare go to the police station alone, and that is why I have come to you. At this juncture, I could not think of anyone other than you!'Saloni had started sobbing.

Suman too looked worried, because she knew that Saloni's apprehension was correct. What if the police proved charges and assembled a case against her—the police might use Avinash's call details as circumstantial evidence,she thought.

Even Suman did not have much information about criminal laws and legal procedures, so the only way was to go to the police station with Saloni and face the music.

A stern faced policewoman in a khaki dress, carrying a red and a blue band with three stars on her shoulder, and a brass buckle belt matching her uniform, made them follow her to a place marked Waiting/Visitor's lounge. The waiting area was outside the room of the ACP in-charge of the women's cell.

'Madam is handling this because it is a high profile case, and these days she is also looking after additional charge, so you might have to wait for some time till she is back from her round,' the lady officer said in a harsh voice and left.

Suman picked up a copy of the daily kept for visitors and turned its pages, while Saloni dried her eyes wet with tears of remorse. Suman repeated words of solace to calm her, but Saloni's uneasiness was increasing with every passing moment. That half-an-hour of waiting time was like a punishment of years for Saloni.

Saloni looked at her wristwatch. 'Suman, what if we have to wait even after dusk? I can see all hell breaking loose at home. How will I face Mom?'

'Don't worry Saloni, in that case, I shall drop you home and will answer Kavita Masi's questions.'

This reduced Saloni's stress a bit.

While speaking to Saloni, Suman felt someone's firm grip on her shoulder, and instantly turned her head to see who it was.

It was difficult for her to believe her eyes.

'Tanu, how come you are here?'

But her uniform and sparkling star with an emblem on her shoulder answered all of Suman's questions. She exulted, 'What luck Tanu, so you are the ACP!' Her heart swelled with happiness. It was difficult for Suman to believe her eyes because she was meeting her high school best friend after a long gap of years. And some of the worries concerning Saloni had also eased.

The ACP in charge was Tanveer Kaur.

'But what brought you here to the police station?' asked Tanveer, leading Suman and Saloni to her room to make them comfortable.

Suman narrated Saloni's story to Tanveer. After patiently listening to her, Tanveer said, 'Don't worry Saloni, you are as dear to me as you are to Suman. I will make sure that your name is off the case register.

It was not just that Saloni was not at fault, but also that it was a matter of the ACP's dearest friend.

TWELVE

A HUGE GRILLED iron gate and the magnificent red brick building of the school was an attractive place because of the enthusiasm packed in the shining eyes of the young girls.

The nuns, addressed as Sisters, in peach colored bordered saris or some wearing a white habit, dedicated themselves to doing service to society. They strived their best to groom the girls for their life ahead. The academic lessons were taught along with the lessons to young girls to grow up into responsible women and good human beings. Their teachings were loaded with tons of advice for a good life; at the other end, there were girls,the classmates, whose giggles and mimicry made life colourful. The girls shared the joys and sorrows of life with their smiles and tears that appeared and vanished as quickly as the fizz in a soda bottle.

The hilarious stories of prankster friends who played tricks, and gorged on other's tiffins till caught with mouths full of food, and warned by the teacher were the anecdotes to be relished later. The greatest joy was securing the highest grade in the class, and the greatest sorrow was getting punishment, and being made to stand outside the classroom, hence missing the chance of doing mischief with friends. At times, Suman used to laugh all alone remembering the silly jokes cracked by classmates, which had the whole class rolling on their desks with infectious laughter.

But, all said and done, only Tanveer was Suman's best friend. Suman shared a deep emotional bond with her. All their secrets were known to each other; their crushes to their changing bra sizes, they would share everything to its minutest detail; they would use the same brand whether it was the sanitary napkins or their specs. They had similar likes and tastes. The only difference they maintained was to have dates with different boyfriends, but that could be possible only in dreams, because moving around with a boy was forbidden during the school day, unlike the present days.

During recess, they would walk hand in hand to Mr Franklin's tuck shop to buy their hot samosas; nibbling samosas they would make their way to the big banyan tree standing in the outermost corner of the hockey field and bare their hearts out to each other.

But, after their high school they had to move with their fathers to their respective job destinations. And, alas, those days were far away from the contemporary world where physical space is digitally minimized in the clouds to minimal cyber space leading to the revolution in communication and connectivity. The social networks and technological gadgets have brought the whole world closer.

'So, are you in touch with all our school friends?' asked Tanveer.

'Well, not all, but quite a few.'

'While we chit-chat let's not forget our favorite samosas from Mr Franklin's shop.' Tanveer phoned her assistant to send tea and samosas to her room.

'Tanu, you have not changed a wee bit!'

'Sumu,' said Tanu, 'Can you forget our priceless time, the memories of our teenage day's at school?' Both Tanveer and Suman felt quite happy to relive their memories. They laughed with the same fervor as they used to do during their school days and Saloni could not help herself from joining in.

THIRTEEN

SUMAN WAS LOOKING for a place to park her car in the parking area, and she saw enough space near Rajan's new sedan, the Audi.

"Let me say Hi to Rajan before I get into my room, or else I might get stuck till afternoon. I will ask him to order for my lunch in his room, and then, during lunch I can invite him home this Sunday and introduce him to Mom and Dad. At least my parents should be made aware of my mind," she thought. Suman had multiple excuses to meet Rajan in the morning.

She headed towards Rajan's department located in the main office building. Her room was in the adjacent building housing customer service and marketing departments.

Rajan and Suman moved to each other's buildings for

matters concerning their work, but the nature of work in the international project had curtailed their mobility because large amounts of paperwork had to be completed in a short span of time.

Suman walked through the reception area receiving greetings from junior staff.

'Hi Ma'am,' the lady sitting at the reception greeted Suman.

'Hi Suzanne! How are you?' Suman reciprocated.

Suman moved ahead with accelerated steps, trying not to waste even a second talking to people she met on the way to his room. But, on hearing her name being called aloud she retraced her steps.

It was Suzanne calling, 'Excuse me, Ma'am!'

Suman came back to check with Suzanne. 'What's the matter Suzanne?'

Suzanne said, 'Ma'am I had to inform you that any document concerning the international project has to be submitted at the reception, to me.'

'Why?' asked Suman.

Suzanne pointed to the notice board which had a paper pinned on it with the information that all office staff working for the international project would be reporting directly to the CEO instead of Rajan Mathur. The related documents and the papers could be submitted at the reception. The information regarding meetings was to be communicated by Suzanne, the reception in-charge.

'When was this notice put up? And where is Rajan?' Suman asked.

'Rajan Sir is not coming to office for almost a week, and the notice, I think, was put up two days back. In fact, I was getting the circular done so that it could be sent to all concerned.'

'But his car is parked in the parking lot.'

'Yeah, that's true, all of us are wondering about the same thing.'

Suman's bewilderment was becoming obvious. She sank on the soft cushioned sofa in the reception lobby and tried to think hard if Rajan had mentioned going out at any point of time.

Nope! Had he told her so, she would have remembered. She took out her mobile and punched speed dial for Rajan. She also had his personal number, which he did not share with anyone else; she was close enough that she had him on speed dial. But both his numbers were 'not reachable'.

What could have happened? Had he put in his papers? Why so? And so suddenly! But why would he keep his mobile off?

And how could things look hunky dory at the office? For the international project, which reigned so high on the company's priority list, an issue like this would be news doing the rounds. Then, how come Rajan being replaced by the CEO did not cause a ripple? Everything had ended so well at the last meeting, then what could be the reason for his absence? And, if he had resigned, or maybe, was fired by the top management, which too was a remote possibility because he was in the good books of all bosses, then why would his car be parked here? Or, did he meet with an accident, or was he not well! In that case, all the office staff would be by his side! Then, what could be the reason?

Suman was confused; her thoughts were in an absolute muddle. What made her sadder was the fact that Rajan did not inform her about his plans, or his absence from office. Rajan vanishing from office without any rhyme or reason, and that too under mysterious circumstances. It raised some eyebrows for sure, but for Suman, it created an emotional void.

FOURTEEN

RAJAN'S ABSENCE CHANGED equations in Suman's life; the agility of her steps changed to a directionless ramble; her face reflected glumness all the time. Going to office was no more exciting. There was an inertia holding her to the bed in the morning, and she thought of excuses like a child not wanting to go to school.

Suman always made preparations for office the previous night—her dress, matching accessories, shoes or sandals... everything. She worked on the minutest details as to how to look good. Rajan did not only disappear from office, but had also taken away Suman's happiness, enthusiasm and excitement. She woke up late in the mornings, and wore to office even the dresses she had kept aside in the rejected lot.

Rajan had kind of eloped with her punctuality and efficiency at work.

In his absence, she found nothing worthwhile to look forward to! Compliments by other colleagues did not make her feel good; rather they reminded her that Rajan was not around and aggravated her pain. Rajan's words of flattery kept echoing in her ears like music making her heart dance to its tunes.

She kept waiting that Rajan would call her up, or at least he would text her that he was fine. But days changed to weeks and a month passed by. He did not even figure in talks of colleagues; it was out of sight out of mind for them. But for Suman, he was there in her heart. She could not forget him.

It was 9 o'clock in the morning. Suman was lazing around on the swing in her balcony, lost in thoughts. Savita came out to clear the garbage from the dustbin kept in the balcony, and was surprised to see Suman still not ready for office.

'Suman, what happened? Are you not getting late for office? Do you know what the time is?' asked Savita.

Suman replied, 'Mamma, please call up my office and tell them I'm not well. I am not going to office today.'

'What's happened to you Suman?' Savita came closer and placed her hand on her forehead. Suman's forehead felt normal.

'Mom, I'm fine. Just feeling a bit tired.'

'You have been working too hard for the project. And that's why you need a break. By the way, is your project over?' Savita asked.

Suman always seemed excited about the project, and she had been talking about it to her parents in great detail.

Suman replied lackadaisically, 'Mom my part of the work is over; now it is for the top bosses to finalize the project.'

Savita tried to look convinced but a mother's heart always knows better.

'If you are saying so, it must be! But your grim face is telling clearly that something is wrong.'

'Mom, I told you, I am not feeling well. That's it.'

'Shall we see a doctor, in that case?'

'No Mom, a little rest will do!'

Savita nodded and moved to the kitchen to finish her remaining work.

The phone in the living room was ringing for quite some time, but Suman remained engrossed in her thoughts. Finally, Savita had to rush from the kitchen to take the call. Suman moved to her room while Savita was talking on the phone. She bolted her door, and did not inquire as to who had called up as she always did.

Saloni had called up to check about Suman, and once

she knew that Suman was home she told Savita that she was coming to their house.

Savita was quite perplexed at her daughter's behaviour. Why is she being so irresponsible and indifferent? She thought of talking to Suman to find out what was wrong with her. But then she thought she would let Saloni come and handle it.'

Savita knew that Suman could not resist her best friend and cousin, Saloni, and she alone could manage Suman's mood.

Saloni reached before Savita could wind up her work in the kitchen. She bubbled with energy, and her face glowed with excitement; she seemed in a hurry to give some news, or maybe gossip.Even before Savita could utter a word, she had already headed towards Suman's room and was banging on the door.

Suman opened the door and let her in.

'Suman! Hey, what's wrong baby? Why is your face looking as long as a fiddle?'asked Saloni with surprise.

Suman was taken aback! "What is Saloni doing here in the morning?" she thought. But she tried to welcome her with a smile.

'Come! Come in Saloni!' And she made her sit beside her on the bed. 'Saloni, did you not have classes today?'

Saloni chuckled, 'No darling!'

'Ok!'

'But why do you have a face like a wet weekend? Why no office today? And your most important project deadlines, what happened to that? Is that project over?'Saloni asked in a non-stop prattle.

'Not really, Saloni!'

'Then what, Suman?'

'I am not well. Just that! You tell me. What's the good news?' Suman asked trying to bring cheer back on her face.

'Not until you prove that you trust me as much as I trust you. Because I know you're lying! I can read your face, and it clearly says that you are suffering from symptoms of heartbreak!' Suman kept quiet, looking blankly at the wall.

'Suman, I know you are not the kind of person who wears her heart on her sleeve, but if you can't even share what's bothering you, then I wonder what's the point in our being friends anymore.'Saloni looked upset and collected her bag to leave.

At that Suman broke down. She narrated the tale about Rajan, in vivid detail, from the first encounter to his sudden disappearance. Even Saloni became quiet after listening to her story.

'Really strange Suman!'And like a seasoned analyst she commented, 'Suman, had you said yes to him on the day he took you out for lunch, he might have known your mind.

Maybe he thought of settling down with some other girl after he did not get any reply from you. And maybe he will come to you one day to introduce his wife.'

Perhaps, what Saloni said was right! Suman thought. 'But what shall I do, Saloni? I have failed in my attempts to convince my mind to leave his thoughts behind and move ahead.'

'I can understand Suman, but you have no other option! You have got to let go and move ahead in life. You need to trust destiny, and accept to walk on the path that is shown by your fate. Maybe god has planned something better for you.'

And Saloni's sermons did work. Suman wiped her tears, as she tried to feel better. Certainly, she wasn't healed completely, but Saloni's words did have an impact.

She recovered from the pain gripping her heart and remembered something.

'Saloni, you came to share some good news, isn't it?'

'Yeah!' Saloni blushed.

'Tell me! Who is the lucky fellow?' Suman asked teasingly, trying to lighten the mood.

'Suman, I seriously can't believe it! I fell in love with him at first sight.'

'Hey! Wait a minute! I hope your 'he' is not another Avinash!'

'No Suman. Prashant is Mum and Dad's choice for

me as my life partner. And we have only Skyped with each other so far.'

'Then how are you sure that he is the right choice.'

'I don't know Suman! But something tells me that he is the person! Mum and Dad knew about him from quite some time, even before he went to the US. Most amazingly, his uncle and aunt are our neighbors, and he came to spend his holidays with his cousins there. His parents sent his proposal through our neighbors because he had been my secret admirer since his school days. And it's so strange that I never noticed him noticing me. But when I saw him on the screen, I fell for him at first sight.'Saloni whisked away the bangs from her forehead to show more clearly her radiant face, and Suman swore that any other boy too would have fallen for her had he seen her at that moment.

'Oh my Saloni! When his thoughts make you look so pretty, how spectacular will you look when he is present before you?' Saloni pinched Suman. 'Ah! okay, but tell me, can you leave all of us and stay in the US forever?'

'No Suman, Prashant is currently working on a project that would be over in two years, and then he has plans of coming back to India.'

'That is good!'

'But currently he is very busy and he could manage to get leave only for a week. So, all ceremonies have to get over in that one-week's time, including the ring ceremony. I think he has even talked about my passport to my folks because he wants me to fly with him straight after marriage.'

'Wow, Saloni. This is called a match made in heaven. I'm so happy for you my dear!'

'Suman, nothing was possible without you. Love you for everything.'

FIFTEEN

SUMAN NEEDED A break. And Saloni's marriage was a good excuse. She took a week off from office. It was not for mere participation, because she formed a part of Saloni's extended family and was bound to undertake some responsibilities for organizing the ceremony. The marriage function had to take place at the Sarins' family home in Meerut.

Kavita, Saloni's mother, assigned the task of arranging the trousseau to Suman. Saloni and Suman would be out for the complete day to shop for Saloni's clothes—from the mega malls to the traditional stores to even the small shops in narrow lanes specializing in zari and silk. Suman tried to give her whole-hearted participation in shopping.

Every passing day brought the day of marriage closer.

Most of the guests were expected to reach a day before. And for that reason, Suman was made to share Saloni's room so that the arrival of guests did not disturb her.

The mellifluous notes of the flute recital combined with the fragrance of fresh flowers heaped up for the decoration of the house, and the rich aroma of sweets and food had rejuvenated the surrounding with their unique blend. The crowd of young guests manifested their energy by dancing till late into the nights. But, as someone has rightly said, "Happiness lies within not without." And Saloni and Suman both proved it right; Saloni's buoyant mood and Suman's somber face reflected their state of mind.

Unlike a traditional Indian bride, becoming coy at the mere mention of marriage, Saloni looked confident and bubbly. She peeped into every room to check whether the guests were comfortable, even joining them and bursting into laughter at family jokes! Suman reluctantly followed Saloni everywhere.

Amidst all the hustle-bustle of activities, Saloni did not miss a chance to connect to her beau, either on phone or through Internet for chat sessions. And when there was only a day left for the wedding, Saloni could not steal a single moment from her hyper-busy, ceremonies packed day, Prashant called up. After a long day of waiting to hear her sweet, melodious voice he drove towards her house and called her up from just two kms away.

Saloni covered the mouthpiece of her mobile and whispered to Suman, 'Suman can you please be on the lookout and inform me if someone is coming towards our room. I don't want my cousins to make fun of me! They will tease me that we are getting impatient for each other. And that we really are!' she said, winking at Suman.

Suman agreed with a smile and moved out of the room to the patio. The decorations were now complete. The strands of flowers and strings of multicoloured bulbs were used profusely for decoration. Suman walked barefoot on the grass, with small steps, inspecting the lighting arrangements. The lights and darkness alternated from one wall to another. The tiny, multicolored bulbs flickered into various designs, the fragrance of flowers mingled with that of blossoms in the garden and filled the surroundings with a scent that could enrapture the soul. But, it was still not enough to get Suman out of the depths of despair. She walked inattentively, trampling the dried leaves that had fallen on the grass from the trees along the house's periphery. Without realizing, she reached the mandap prepared towards the end of the lawn.

It was like a quiet hour amidst the entire day's sequence of activities, and the environs had taken a cue to appear calm and still—even the air showed minimum movement.

And that made the surrounding sound waves become dominant; even the slightest breeze made an audible rustle. Just then the creaking sound of the iron main gate with its screeching hinge and the squelching sound of footsteps made Suman take an about turn to look in the direction of the approaching footsteps.

All she could see was something like a human shape approaching the patio; with quickened steps, she moved closer to the shadow, lest it did any harm to Saloni. Her heart felt like it would burst with the heightened pace of her heartbeat, but she was only concerned for Saloni at that moment. And as she moved closer, the silhouette changed to a masculine form. On seeing Suman approaching him, his steps too moved towards her. She halted for a moment and rubbed her eyes, but she could not see the face of the person. She had already checked by pinching herself that she was not in trance. But who could be walking inside the house at this hour of night?

And she started getting gooseflesh thinking that it was Rajan's soul coming to meet her; maybe Rajan was no more in this world! Her mind and body worked as separate entities; mind still working to confirm the credentials of the silhouette and body poised to ensure safety of both Saloni and her own self. She started running to reach Saloni's room and bumped into the shadow headlong.

'Oh!'

'Ouch!'

And the two sets of eyes met—Suman holding her forehead which struck against the gold plated kurta buttons of the shadow that had evolved into a man. The young man looked as if he had committed some sin because bumping into his wide strong chest had hurt her.

'Oh! I'm so sorry ma'am! Are you alright?' His voice appeared concerned.

'I'm fine! It was my mistake. I just got scared! It's ok, I am perfectly fine.' Suman said to make him feel comfortable.

Suman had a bruise on her forehead, which was bleeding. The young man placed his hand on the injured forehead and rubbed it gently. It made Suman feel better. But the touch of his hand made an impact; Suman could not know why. The roses had lent their color to her cheeks to make her look flushed.

She held his hand and demurely forced it back away from her and said, 'Thanks! It's ok now. I feel better.'

Saloni too had moved out of her room to look for Suman, after finishing her talk with Prashant. For a moment, she too stood still looking at both Suman and the young man near the patio!

And she burst into laughter, 'Hey, what are you guys up to? Do you know each other?'

'Saloni…stop kidding!' Saloni's remark made Suman blush and she had to brush off her statement in a slightly firm tone.

By that time Saloni had directed her attention towards the young man. 'Oh bhai! What are you doing here at this hour...?'

Suman felt uncomfortable, so she started moving towards the room.

But Saloni could apprehend Suman's mood; she prevented her from moving inside by holding her hand. 'Where are you going Suman? Come, meet my brother Kunal.'

'Hi!' Suman said.

Kunal reciprocated with a'Hello'. And he started talking to Saloni, as if there was something urgent that had brought him to her in the middle of the night.

Suman, though feeling embarrassed, had to stay with Saloni and hear her conversation.

While Saloni was busy talking to Kunal, Suman found some time to stealthily look at his face. He was a very handsome man with thick brows, long nose and broad jaws. A well-trimmed moustache adorned his fair face. He was tall with good growth of hair on his head. He could woo any lady with his charm. For a few seconds, Suman could not move her eyes away from him.

Saloni was addressing the man as her brother, but how come Suman did not know about Saloni's cousins, both sharing their lineage from their mother's side. They had many common cousins whom she had not met for long, but she knew each one very well. The only possibility could be that the young man was Saloni's relative from her father's side, thought Suman.

Kunal was telling Saloni to go along with him instantly to meet the agent who had to come in the middle of the night to get her signature on the visa form, to ensure she got her visa in time. Prashant and Saloni both wished to fly together to US after their marriage, and because their marriage was a hurriedly planned one, it required bypassing of procedures to meet deadlines. Brig Sarin had exploited his contacts for ensuring that his daughter flew with his son-in-law.

'It's just becoming impossible to connect with you on your mobile. Wonder whom are you busy talking to?' Kunal talked with a mark of authority with Saloni.

'Just cool down, and please make the agent wait for a few more minutes. I will be there with Suman as soon as possible,' she said snapping her fingers.

Kunal said, 'Ok, I shall convey this to Uncle. And don't forget that we are waiting, or else you might get stuck in something unnecessary. And if you fail to show up in time then it will not be possible for you to accompany your hubby to the US.'

'No...no...I am just coming.' Saloni swiftly rushed to her room to put on her slippers.

Suman added with a gentle smile, 'Don't worry I will bring her in time.'

Kunal smiled and said, 'Well, now I can be assured because Saloni hasn't grown up still. Poor Prashant, I'm sure is going to have a tough time with her.' And he went away.

Saloni and Suman held hands and headed towards Kunal's residence which housed half of Sarins' marriage guests, and where the agent waited with Brig Sarin and Kunal in the drawing room. Saloni's father and Kunal were conversing with the agent and Kunal looked more concerned than Brig Sarin regarding the formalities.

Saloni put her signature at the designated places on the form, and once the paperwork was over the agent asked Brig Sarin, 'Sir, if you don't mind can I ask you a personal question?'

Brig Sarin replied quite spiritedly, 'Why not? Please go ahead!'

'Sir, I know that daughters can have their surnames different from their fathers', but why does your son have a surname different from yours? I mean he is Kunal Bhalla and you are Brig Sarin!'

Brig Sarin had a hearty laugh; Kunal too joined him and so did Saloni and Suman. The agent made an attempt to move away, but Brig Sarin signalled him to wait.

It took them a while to control their laughter, and thereafter, Brig Sarin began speaking. 'Is it essential that one has to be related biologically or be related through blood to ensure that one is emotionally close too? Can there not be a relationship which is beyond the blood relationship. Kunal is more than a son for us,' he said patting Kunal on his back. He then encircled his shoulder and brought him near and looked at his face saying, 'Thanks Son—thanks for being better than the best son.'

'Kunal is my friend Bishwajeet's son. And Bishwajeet was more than my own brother for me.'

The face of the agent had a strange look of surprise. When the agent left, Brig Sarin said, 'I feel pity for such narrow thinking people —those who cannot appreciate the essence of human connection which can be beyond flesh and blood.'

SIXTEEN

THE UNBREAKABLE BOND of friendship between Shekhar Sarin and Bishwajeet Bhalla, which started at National Defence Academy, Khadakwasla, was the stuff of legends. They had proved the theory of blood thicker than water completely wrong. Their bond was stronger than even that of brothers.

After his father, Kunal had stepped into his role, further strengthening the ties of that bond, and was performing the duties of a son for Brig Sarin. His wife Kavita too had never made Kunal feel the emptiness created by the death of his father, who had sacrificed his life for the country while performing his duties as part of IPKF mission.

The black iron boxes of the two close chums, with their names Shekhar Sarin and Bishwajeet Bhalla inscribed on them in white, always remained together except for the posting in the IPKF peace mission. This time, Bishwajeet and Shekhar did not get a common posting. The affinity between the two friends was further strengthened when the two ladies, Kavita and Naina, joined them as their wives. Shekhar had played a pivotal role in the marriage of Bishwajeet and Naina.

Bishwajeet married his wife Naina against the wishes of his family. They varied widely in their financial status, and to add to the woes, their castes were also different. Shalabhjeet and Bishwajeet were the two brothers who were heirs to the enormous wealth of land and industry of the Bhalla clan.

Bishwajeet, always a rebel against the mindless distinctions defined by society, joined the Indian Army against the wishes of his family. Whenever he was sanctioned leave, he would return to his parents' home and spend all his time with his brother's children, Tiya and Tarun, whom he adored like his very own.

His days would be packed with plans for the kids, who had a fabulous time with their uncle. They were allowed a free reign all the time except for the two hours they were expected to devote to their studies. Bishwajeet would use that time to keep up with his fitness routine, keeping in line with the stringent army rules.

It was during one of Bishwajeet's visits thatTarun had

to appear for the 8th std examination, and Bishwajeet came to know from the children that their new lady teacher was very nice but also very strict about studies. The children would be busy making merry the entire day, but just before their tuition time they made sure to be in their study room. Bishwajeet's holiday was approaching its end and the children wanted to spend the maximum time with their uncle.

Bishwajeet too made an effort to spend every moment with them in a manner that the time formed part of his happy memories till his next vacation. A popular Disney movie was playing in the town theatre and he had planned a surprise for the kids by taking them for the movie. He ended his exercise session slightly early and came to the kids' study room to take them out.

Seeing their uncle, Tiya and Tarun got restless and to focus on studies became difficult for them.

Naina, their teacher, was perplexed; she was unable to check the kids' enthusiasm at the sight of their uncle, so how could she make them concentrate on their lessons. She had to finish their syllabus for the approaching examination.

Finally, Naina was unable to control herself, and she spoke in her melodious voice. 'Sir, if we as elders are not able to check ourselves how can we expect these children to be disciplined and concentrate on their studies.' She gently chided Bishwajeet, 'I request you to please stop disturbing them during their study time. You can have all the fun you want after they finish their studies.'

Bishwajeet fell head over heels in love with the charming lady. He was quite impressed with her grace and her beauty. Her words fell on Bishwajeet's ears like the music of a flute amidst the sound of bullets in the battlefield. He was rendered speechless and motionless for a few seconds. Though Naina belonged to a sub-caste which stood lower in the caste hierarchy, her manners were more dignified than those of the most sophisticated ladies in his family.

From that day onwards, he used to wait for Naina, sitting in the garden. She was never late by even a minute. He tried to steal a glance at her pretty face from behind the newspaper. He would offer her a cup of tea, after she finished teaching the kids, which she would accept with a little hesitation.

Bishwajeet had refused all his marriage proposals and his parents had given up hope of his marriage.

He detested the traditional marriage, which to him was more of a commercial transaction. The bride was valued on the basis of the dowry she fetched, and the marriage negotiations were based on financial status of the bride and groom. The mutual preference of the two human beings, who had to stay together for the rest of their lives, was not given any importance. A man and a woman would produce offsprings without having slightest concern for each other.

He was just not convinced about this and he termed it an absurdity of life.

He did not know that he would start liking someone so much that he would be willing to spend his entire life with her. Someone whom his heart approved, and whose presence alone made life appear beautiful.

Bishwajeet's leave was about to end, and he would be away to his posting for months again. He longed for her company but did not know how to ask her out.

For two days, Naina did not come to teach the children. Bishwajeet had a good excuse to take the children out for a ride and then to their teacher's home. Tiya, the more talkative of the two, could guide him to the exact route to her teacher's house.

The way to Naina's house was an arduous journey through meandering alleys and streets. There was heavy rain that day, and the excess water had made the drains along the roads overflow and cover the potholes, causing sudden jerks in the old model fiat car.

Driving through the water-logged lanes was difficult for Bishwajeet, but his determination to meet Naina was strong. The children kept their patience—maybe they understood their uncle's liking for their teacher. Tarun kept motivating his uncle, 'Oh uncle, it is the test of your driving skills on these challenging roads, otherwise who cannot drive on smooth well managed roads. We travel daily on these roads to our schools.' And Tiya kept guiding the way to their teacher's house. Finally, he managed to reach Naina's house.

The car came to a halt walloping a big stone near a puddle splashing muddy water all around, and all over the car's outer surface. On hearing the screeching sound of a car, a lady came out of her house.

Seeing the kids, she welcomed them with a smile, and spread her arms calling aloud: 'Tiya, Tarun, come…come!'

The old lady looked graceful in her starched cotton sari which she had worn in a traditional style; the pallu hanging down from across her right shoulder spread elegantly across the bosom, and the left edge was tucked in the petticoat at the back.

'We have come to meet Naina aunty,' the children said eagerly. The lady offered a red carpet welcome to the guests. 'Come, Come,' she responded with the same enthusiasm as the children. She reached near the car and picked up Tiya, the younger of the two, and Tarun held her hand and walked inside the house. It had been ages since Bishwajeet had come to the interior of the city and that too after rains. The entrance of the house was all swampy. The cement plaster of the floor was missing in incongruous patches revealing the earth underneath. The loose earth got mixed with rainwater to make the place muddy.

He had almost forgotten that he too was like these kids before he went to his boarding school. He had never felt uncomfortable in moving through the interior of the town with his parents.

He followed the children into the room. The lady put the navy blue curtain aside. It looked clean but was torn and mended at many places. The grey-cemented floor in the room got clear marks of their footsteps. The children's acquaintance with the lady did not seem to be new. Naina's mother had been a familiar face at Bishwajeet's house, helping with cooking and preparing snacks, on occasions, and the children seemed to be quite fond of her.

Naina's mother lifted a corner of her sari and dusted the seat of one of the wooden chairs, which was woven with white plastic wire. This was the best furniture she could offer to her guests. The other chair had its plastic wire broken in the center and all the strings hung loose. There was a divan covered with an old bed sheet exposing the mattress which was hand sewed by joining the incongruous and heterogeneous patches of clothes—not for making some design but these were pieces of rags put to best use. Two earthen oil wicks illuminated the room, one kept on the wooden ledge before a framed photo, and the other on a four-legged wooden stool kept near the chair on which Bishwajeet sat.

The lady took the children to the inner room to meet their Naina aunty.

In the dim light, Bishwajeet threw a quick glance around the room and his eyes got fixed on the framed photograph on the ledge. He got up from his chair and went near the photograph and all the fading memories of his schooldays started becoming vivid and clear. The photo was of his school headmaster with a garland hanging around it.

Mastersaab used to teach children the fundamentals of English grammar and tell them motivational stories during their early childhood, hence laying the foundation of values and igniting the spark to do well in life. He, along with most children of the area had attended that school before going to the boarding. In the school that lacked even the basic infrastructure to conduct classes, people like 'mastersaab', as he was respectfully addressed, dedicated himself to improving the quality of education of small town children. It was due to him that most of the students, whom he had taught in their primary and secondary classes, were quite successful and well settled in life.

People like mastersaab created such a place of education that no school with magnificent building structures and modern gadgets could rival.

'What will you have, tea or sharbat?' The lady's voice brought Bishwajeet's flow of thoughts to a stop. The old lady had not forgotten the hospitality deserved by a guest despite the financial strain.

'No…no nothing, thanks, actually these children were missing their Naina aunty a lot, so I brought them here,' said Bishwajeet. 'But what happened to mastersaab?' he asked. 'I didn't know Naina was his daughter.'

The lady did not want to reveal her family's problems to a stranger, so she tried to divert his attention. 'You have come to our house for the first time. We will talk about other things later. Naina is suffering from high fever from past two days and so she could not go to take classes. I have brought the medicine from the chemist. It has made her feel better and probably by tomorrow she should be fit enough to take the classes both at the school and her tuitions.' Saying this, the lady again tried to make a move out of the room to get some refreshment for her guests. Bishwajeet could read her mind. He tried to stop her from getting into any kind of formality.

'Naina will be happy to see you all here. I know this place is not worth your coming to, but since you have come, please have something before you leave.'

Bishwajeet, showing his humility, said, 'Chachi, please don't say this! This would mean showing disrespect to our most revered teacher! And by the way, what's wrong with this place? This place is a temple of learning.' Pointing towards the picture on the wall he said, 'Many more like me owe our career and success to him. He laid the foundation of the career of so many students.' Mastersaab was an MA in English literature. He had forgone lectureship in Lucknow university and had settled for a job as a school teacher because he wanted to improve the standard of English of the small town children, who lagged behind only due to their improper knowledge of the language.

The lady put her hand on Bishwajeet's head and blessed him, 'Always be happy in your life. How many people admit this today? Despite having all the best things in life your head is not inflated with vanity and pride. God will always help you my son!'

By that time, Naina and the children joined Bishwajeet in the room. Naina looked slightly pale but smiled and greeted him.

Naina displayed no signs of her poverty, rather her eyes had the sparkle of self-respect and happiness. She made use of her learning to look after her mother by working as a teacher and taking tuitions.

Bishwajeet took an immediate decision. The lady came in with homemade sharbat for everybody. Naina was busy talking to the kids.

Lifting the glass of sharbat, he said, 'Chachi I am not good at talking, so I will express myself in straightforward words.'

'Sure! But what happened?' the lady asked. 'You don't need to hesitate to ask for anything from me.'

'Chachiji, I want to marry your daughter Naina, if she has no problems!'

'What!' Both mother and daughter said in the same voice!

Naina said, 'Please don't make fun of our poverty.'

'What! How can I make fun if I say that I want to marry you?' asked Bishwajeet.

The old lady said, 'We don't match your standard in any respect. We belong to different castes and I also don't have any money to offer to you and your family that you deserve. In fact, I can hardly afford anything for my daughter's marriage.'

'Money, why money? Marriages are associations of souls where the prime consideration should be acceptance of each other as life partners, and I am well settled, getting a decent salary in a decent job, then why do I need your money?'

'You are not aware of the antagonism you will have to face for this marriage,' said Naina's mother.

'I don't care; I am ready to face everything. In Naina,I can see the image that I wish to see in my life partner. And it's I who will decide who should be my wife, not anybody else.' Bishwajeet did not budge in his conviction.

Naina and her mother were left stunned. Naina said,

'But I cannot leave my mother alone. Who will look after her if I am not here?'

'She can come and stay with us,' he said. 'Like you are her daughter, can she not consider me her son?' Bishwajeet said, looking into her eyes.

'Son, it's a result of some good deeds of my past that you have appeared as an angel in our life. If Naina gets a husband like you, all my worries would be resolved. And to look after myself is not much of a hassle as I get the pension of my late husband, and the amount is enough for me to live.'

Bishwajeet did not know how to convey his decision to his family, but Tiya did the job by spilling the beans. She narrated the story to everyone in the family. It was not only the people in the house but the whole town knew about Bishwajeet's marriage to Naina.

Everyone in the family was against Bishwajeet, though each had a different reason. Charu, Shalabhjeet's wife was furious to know about the marriage plans. She had planned for Bishwajeet's marriage with her snooty sister, Prachi.

Bishwajeet's parents opposed the marriage because Naina did not belong to their caste, and also because Naina's mother was treated almost like a maid in the family. Whatever concern they had shown to her after the death of Mastersaab was to keep their family esteem of being called philanthropic. They could never imagine having any relationship with her. They had closed their eyes to the goodness of her father, who was highly respected by one and all in the town.

Bishwajeet stuck to his guns in the face of all antagonism. The resolve he had made would not be changed for anyone in the world, not even his parents whom he loved a lot. He knew that his parents were wrong and were blinded by power and money.

His low profile marriage ceremony was performed in the Ashtavinayaka temple attended only by Naina's mother, his friend Shekhar Sarin and few of Naina's friends. Thereafter, Naina's mother went to live in her village. Bishwajeet took care of his mother-in-law till her final days; they visited her regularly and often brought her along to stay with them.

After his marriage, he did not keep in touch with his parents. He could have inherited enormous property from them for they owned acres of land and a few industries.

SEVENTEEN

TIME HAD FLOWN since then. The two families spent their good and bad times together.

The Bhallas and Sarins had many postings at the same place, or at the most in nearby areas. The families used to spend most of the weekends together; either in one of their houses or on an excursion to surrounding places.

The IPKF was the first such posting when Bishwajeet had to part ways with his family and friend Shekhar for a long period of time. Shekhar Sarin still remembered how he had insisted that Bishwajeet should somehow get his posting in IPKF(Indian Peace Keeping Force) changed, and Bishwajeet had said that he would not miss such an opportunity at any cost.

'But, Bhalla, you know that wherever we have served we have served together, and god has been helping us in keeping our promise that we would be together wherever we go. It is the first time since our commissioning that we will be serving at separate places.'

Bishwajeet had said, 'Grow up Shekhar! Now we are in the rank of senior officers. And being Colonels we cannot behave like we did when we started our career as lieutenants. If life demands action, we must act accordingly and move out of the comfort of doing only what we wish to.'

Shekhar had said, 'Then let me join you and request the authorities for my posting in the mission.' But Bishwajeet had said, 'Look Shekhar, if one of us is with our families to take care of them we both can do our jobs well. You please be here and take care of both the families.'

Col Bishwajeet Bhalla died the death of a martyr while serving in the mission and Shekhar Sarin and his wife left no stone unturned in filling the void in Naina and Kunal's life.

Many a times Shekhar had visited Bishwajeet's parents during their training days and shared a very good rapport with them. Though Bishwajeet did not display his emotions for his parents, but he never forgot them even for a moment. He always remained a concerned son, and took care of his old and ailing parents, if not by himself, then through his friend Shekhar.

Shekhar and his wife Kavita went with the news of Bishwajeet's death to his parents, and it had given them a great shock. They thought it was God's way of making them pay dearly for not accepting a gentle soul as their daughter-in-law.

They realised their mistake after meeting Naina and Kunal, and without any loss of time, accepted their son's family. It was the only memory remaining of their lost son. The reconnection, also became possible due to the efforts of the Sarin family. They began considering Naina like their daughter. Many people had suggested toNaina to get married again, but she savoured memories of the days spent with her husband. She considered Bishwajeet as a hero in the true sense, the country's brave soldier, a lover and an ideal husband, and a very good father.

Naina looked after her in-laws and did everything to ensure that they did not miss their son. She remembered every detail that Bishwajeet shared with her that made his parents happy. Naina, the cause of rift between the parents and son became the conduit of love and concern after his death. Bishwajeet's parents could do nothing except feel sorry for being so late in accepting their son's family.

Shekhar never forgot the promise he had made to his friend of looking after his family in his absence. Both he and his wife Kavita acted as pillars of strength for Naina and Kunal.

Considering the poor state of education in Meerut, they had kept Kunal with them for his higher education. Kunal's desire to pursue higher education would not have been possible, had he been staying in Meerut. He could accomplish his dream of doing his Engineering and getting his MBA from Asian School of Management, Manila with the help of Sarins. He always felt indebted to the Sarin family. Kunal held Brig Sarin and Kavita in very high esteem.

EIGHTEEN

MARRIAGES, ESPECIALLY IN India, are the time to rejoice and revel, for all relatives and friends. The extent of extravaganza depends upon the social and financial status of the person hosting the function.

Saloni, the only daughter of the Sarins was the apple of their eye. She was a female child born in the Sarin family after three generations. Shekhar was the only child of his parents, and his father had two brothers. Unlike the birth of daughters in Indian families, Saloni's birth was celebrated as a blessing from God. The day Shekhar held her in his hands as a little baby he cherished a dream; the dream of a grand wedding for his daughter. Kavita and Shekhar had decided to make their daughter's marriage the most memorable event for everyone, most of all for their precious child.

Marriages, that too Indian marriages are grand social events calling for immense organizational capability. Brig Sarin's capabilities were put to test in his own daughter's marriage. His age had put a question mark on his efficiency. This social function is incomplete without friends and family; the bigger the list of attendees, greater is the challenge.

To ease the task of Brig Sarin, there was only one person whom he could depend on and that was Kunal. Saloni's marriage was a testing ground for Kunal too, because even if not biologically, he was Saloni's brother in all other aspects. There could not have been a better opportunity for Naina and Kunal, if not to repay, then at least to show their appreciation to the family that had done so much for them.

Kunal was so engrossed in the activities that he even missed having his food. Many of the relatives were heard saying, 'We didn't know that Shekhar had a son too.' Or, 'His son is very good natured.' Others would say, 'He is so gentle and smart…Shekhar is lucky…'

Naina kept listening to the opinions being voiced about her son and would smile to herself saying, 'After all he is his father's son!'

Kunal's grandparents were also present on the occasion. Though they were there to attend Saloni's marriage, they could also be heard discussing their grandson Kunal's marriage.

With bodies that had become frail, the wrinkled skin

around the eyes and the deteriorating body systems refusing to function with any coordination, the grandparents had just one dream left to be fulfilled—to celebrate the marriage of their grandson with the fervour they missed at the time of his father's marriage.

The selection of the girl was left to Naina and Kunal. Kunal's granny was often heard saying to Naina, 'Naina you have taken such good care of both of us which is difficult even for a daughter to do. Now just fulfill one more wish of ours, get a bride for Kunal just like you—beautiful and with a gentle soul.'

After meeting Suman, Naina had a feeling that she was the best match for her son. Naina could make out that it was Suman who would permeate her son's life like the sweet fragrance from fresh flowers of the spring season, rejuvenating and enlivening her son's world. Suman had become the cynosure of Naina's eyes. She had been minutely observing her. Her pretty face, her mannerisms and the way she gelled with all the guests around, whether it was the family members or the workers, she ensured no one missed their food or the fun at the ceremony.

Naina briskly walked all around the Sarins' house to look for her son. Before talking to Suman and her parents she wanted to know Kunal's mind; after all, it was he who had to spend his life with Suman.

After looking into the corridors, she walked across the guest room to Kunal's room. Sitting on a chair with its back facing the entrance, Kunal looked like he was engrossed in something before him. Naina pushed the door to open it. She walked softly towards Kunal so as not to disturb his concentration. Moving closer, she looked at the mobile phone in Kunal's hand. To her surprise it had Suman's photo with a beautiful expression.

Kunal had been secretly following Suman and clicking her photos whenever she looked happy and was smiling. She smiled to herself and retraced her steps. She had got the answer. Before she could reach the door, Kunal called out, 'Ma…you here?' He had stood up from the chair with his hand holding the mobile at his back.

Naina smilingly did an about turn to face him. 'Kunal, I am going to talk to Suman's parents.'

Kunal understood what Naina meant. He hugged her saying, 'My mom knows the best!'

Naina patted his head and said, 'Thanks for supporting my decision.'

Kunal and Suman were the busy bees coordinating and putting things in order for the marriage ceremony. They crossed paths many times with their eyes talking.

NINETEEN

UNDER THE MARQUEE full of people witnessing Saloni's marriage rituals, with guests sipping coffee on a pleasant autumn night, and the live rendition by a music troupe of the local marriage songs, Naina and Savita sat next to each other gazing adoringly at Kunal and Suman. When the two of them, Suman and Kunal, were attending to their assigned duties in the marriage, destiny was busy planning their wedding.

The embryo's connection to the mother, through the umbilical cord, once detached makes the infant exist as an independent individual. But mothers for their entire life fail to accept that their child has grown up enough to look after his needs. Both the mothers discussed the merits of their children proving them to be the best in this world.

Naina placed her proposal before Suman's parents and they readily agreed. They had seen their daughter happy in the company of Kunal. Still, Savita asked Suman about the proposal, and Suman could not say no to it. Her parents did whatever they could to ensure that she was happy. She could not punish her parents by taking a vow against marriage, just because of what had happened with Rajan.

Savita held the hennaed hands of her daughter, caressing them with her gentle touch and remembered her soft hands with layers of fat when she was a baby. Suman's birth had blessed her with the joy of motherhood; the sweetness of the feeling had taken away all the blues of the labour pain. The sight of her beautiful baby had made her forget the tortures and the afflictions of her mom-in-law. Savita remembered the entire scene at the time of Suman's birth…

TWENTY

AFTER THE NIGHT long drizzling, the weather in the early morning was pleasant. Amidst heavy downpour, the clear sky was a rarity. Like the unwanted guests whose needless and untimely presence spoils the day-to-day routine of the house, the rains came unannounced and continued without interruptions, the temperament of nature remained highly unpredictable.

Savita was in endless labour pain, in a small dark room, along with the traditional midwife, Bedamia, as she was known in the town. Bedamia was well known for her prowess at relieving ladies from their pain and making them deliver healthy babies with ease.

Savita was begging Bedamia, 'Please ask my husband to call my parents.'

Bedamia tried to console Savita saying, 'Don't worry, things will soon be all right. Let me ask Shravanbabu to call the lady doctor. I won't be able to handle your case, it is getting complicated.'

Shravan's mother, Premadevi, busy as a hibernating bear, was sitting in the verandah outside Savita's labour room with the next door neighbour. She overheard all the conversation between Savita and Bedamia.

Before Shravan could decide to get a doctor for his wife, his mother acted. She requested the neighbour's boy to go and call her daughter-in-law's parents. Premadevi wanted to capitalise on the opportunity by calling Savita's parents; this would help her wash her hands of the expenses of her daughter-in-law's pregnancy, and also earn her a good name as a considerate mother-in-law.

Mrs Savant, Savita's mother, was making preparations for the arrival of their grandchild. Mr Savant was turning over leaves of Savita's marriage album. He heaved a sigh and said, 'With Savita's marriage all our responsibility is over. It seems nothing more remains to be done in life.'

Mrs Savant, humming a lullaby, was concentrating on stitching cloth napkins for her soon to be grandchild. She asked her husband, 'Have you drawn out money for a gold chain for Savita's child? Since it is her first child we will have to gift some gold, as we have done for our other grandchildren.'

The sound of the doorbell surprised the old couple. 'Who can come to meet us in such a rain so early in the morning?' said Mrs Savant.

She called her maid to open the door. The sad face of the boy narrated half the news. He told them that their daughter was in unbearable pain and that Bedamia was not able to handle her condition, which had become quite complicated. She had not been able to deliver after eight hours of continuous labour pains. Hearing this Mrs Savant's eyes were full of tears. She said, 'Couldn't they afford a lady doctor for Savita's delivery; the ignorance of the midwife will kill my daughter.'

Mr Savant gestured to her to be quiet and asked her to get ready to go to their daughter. The rain had stopped by then. Mr Savant in the meanwhile called his old trusted servant, Ram Chander, and asked him to get their family doctor Aruna directly to Savita's in-laws house.

The anguish of a mother for her daughter was inexplicable even to Mr Savant. The best means of communication, a bus that could be called faintly better than dilapidated, was the only means of transport available to reach their daughter at the earliest. The old bus running at its best speed would take at least three hours to reach their daughter's place.

Mrs Savant's heart was wailing and tears flowed from her eyes. She kept praying in her heart all through the jarring bus ride. She told her husband, 'How my daughter, who did not know the pain of the prick of a thorn must be bearing pain for all these hours.' Mr Savant could not even shed tears for his daughter.

They reached their daughter's house, knocked at the door, and waited for the response. Soon, they were joined by Shravan's parents.

"Pranam samdhi, samdhinjee." This exchange of salutation was the best courtesy offered to Savita's parents. Despite this, they did not utter a word against Shravan or his parents, lest it worsen their daughter's condition at her in-law's house.

Shravan's mother spoke with affectation, 'It is unbearable to see Savita in so much pain… we were thinking of calling the lady doctor, but we are not aware of any such doctor. You know the last time it was in Phagunia's…you know Phagunia, my sister's daughter, delivery case. They had called the lady doctor and she made the matter so complicated.' Mrs Savant could not listen to her excuses and went inside to be with her daughter.

Mr Savant said, 'Don't worry! I have already sent for our family doctor; she should be here any moment. She is quite a capable doctor, and I think the whole town is aware of that!' He said, 'I think when we can avail of better facilities why should we risk any mishap?' Shravan and his father nodded, but Shravan's mother twisted her face and without a word went away suggesting that she did not like the idea.

Ram Chander was getting old so he asked his son Saryu to hitch him a ride to the doctor's residence. The road was clogged with water. The innumerable potholes were barely visible because of the water logging. Saryu decided to take his father through the fields along the railway tract. Ram Chander was not in favor of going that way, as it was the time when men and women who had come to work on the new factory project would be attending to their natural call, in the lush green surroundings along the railway tract. Ram Chander covered his eyes.

A strong gust of wind swayed the trees, dropping off the water collected on the leaves. People hiding behind the bushes as their cloak were exposed to the naked gaze of passers by. As the trees moved with the wind, Saryu could steal glances at some pretty young girls, who were collecting the branches and tree twigs for fuel. He would wink at those girls with a naughty whistle and a smile, to which the girls responded by covering their faces with their duppatta.

Ram Chander, sitting on the front rod of his son's cycle, kept his eyes closed all through the way till he reached the doctor's house.

Had it not been for Mr Savant's order, Ram Chander would never have agreed to go. Not obeying his master's order was almost like committing a sin for him. Mr Savant cared for Ram Chander and his family like his own. The cycle, which both father and son were riding was also a gift from Mr Savant. He had purchased the cycle for Saryu on his passing his matric exam.

Saryu applied the brakes on his cycle and announced that they had reached the doctor's house. Ram Chander felt relaxed accompanying the doctor in her car to show her the way. When the doctor arrived, Savita heaved a sigh of relief.

A husky voice filled the verandah, 'Baby is born!' The next sentence that 'a baby girl is born' filled the environment with silence. Birth of a baby girl means a life filled with toils and travails for the whole family, including the girl. Mrs Savant felt sad thinking that her daughter too would have tough days in looking after her granddaughter. She lifted the baby in her arms and fondly looked at her. The baby's enchanting face moved her deeply. She said, 'Baby girl, the goddess Laxmi has come to us.'

TWENTY-ONE

SAVITA WAS THINKING that the time had come to send Suman away from her to her in-law's place. It would be a tearful moment, bidding farewell to her daughter but this time the tears would be of joy.

Savita's own experience with her sly and complaining mother-in-law always made her pray that her daughter should not undergo harsh treatment in her marital house.

Her dream of a loving home for their daughter would be met in Kunal's family. She was fortunate to have someone like Naina as Suman's mother-in-law. Savita wanted a boy who would respect her daughter for her qualities and would love her for what she was, and not the bank balance or assets that she would take along to her husband's house.

Suman was blossoming into a beautiful bride to begin a new journey of her life. Her walk through the sequined passage with Kunal would lead her to a new world of married life and happiness.

She would have a companion with whom she would experience all the ups and downs of life and share all her joys and sorrows.

TWENTY-TWO

AFTER SALONI'S MARRIAGE, there was one more session of hustle-bustle for the guests, and that was for Suman's marriage. The turn of events had made Suman gradually put a thick curtain between her past with Rajan and her present with Kunal.

Though she sometimes suffered bouts of pain in her heart, but destiny helped her spread a soothing unguent on her soul. Whenever she was alone, her mind would delve into the past and memories of the time she had spent with Rajan would resurface. But, she had learnt to accept the present. And the present was as beautiful as Kunal, a suave groom with a genteel family.

Suman sat on a bed in an artistically decorated room; fresh mogra, roses and orchids filled the room with their fragrance. She was getting mesmerized by the delicate aroma of scented candles and beautiful flowers. For a moment she thought she was in paradise. Her thoughts changed to reality as Kunal was bolting the door of the room while she was busy admiring the ambience. He switched the lights off, and the room was lit only by the light of candles.

He came near Suman, close enough for her breath to catch in her throat. He held her hand and raised it to his lips; the heat of his lips became too much for her and she closed her eyes. She felt a warm gentle touch on her eyes as Kunal kissed both her eyes murmuring, 'Don't save me from drowning in your beautiful ocean of love.'

He hugged her and she felt like she had no control over her body. The drapes slipped off her skin, and her breast was under his tough masculine clasp. Their perfumes mingled, and waves of beautiful emotions were aroused with the heat of Kunal's bare body on hers.

Suman and Kunal were lost in their new world of enchantment; they were awake the whole night, and were forced to leave their bed only when the birds began to sing announcing the beginning of a new day, a new life for both of them.

She clung to his wide chest. Her fingers played with his chest hair. She asked, 'Kunal will we always love each other the way we do now?'

'Do you have any doubts about that?' asked Kunal. 'And Suman, the same question I put to you. Will your love for me change or will it be the way it is today?' Suman looked bewildered for a second. Probably, she did not know the answer, and to save herself she moved away from Kunal, feigning annoyance and said, 'I will not talk to you.'

Kunal pulled her back and held his ears saying, 'Sorry ma'am, no kidding. My darling is quite touchy!' he jested.

Suman was back in her position half smiling and half in tears. They wished to be in each other's company for some more time, but Suman said to Kunal, 'Let me get ready because the guests are around, and surely Mom will wish that we join them for breakfast.'

Suman was right! Just then there was a call which Kunal answered. 'Mom, we are getting ready. Suman will join you in 15 minutes and me soon after.' He was looking at Suman for confirmation to which she nodded.

'Good job! How did you know what Mom was thinking?'

Suman smiled saying, 'So you trust my sixth sense now!'

'Sure madam!'

Suman was filled with a newfound ecstasy and Kunal was in an unusually good mood. They were both not spared any time to be together as all the relatives wanted to spend time with the bride and carry with them beautiful memories of the marriage. Suman's patience was tested as every person had a list of similar questions for her, which she had to answer individually. It was like a ragging session where she was expected to respond with a sweet smile hiding her discomfiture. Kunal's mother came to make sure that all the relatives were through with their breakfast.

She had to drive away the guests encircling Suman. 'Girls and ladies, please allow Suman some time to rest. Can't you understand that she must be tired of your questions?' And the group got up laughing and dispersed.

Suman felt hungry, but before she could ask someone to show her the way to the kitchen, the servant came with the breakfast tray. It had two plates arranged with scrumptious snacks; hot puffed matar kachoris, aloo sabzi and some sweets. The breakfast was for Suman and Kunal. And Naina followed the servant.

'Suman, whatever you need you just call the servant by pressing the bell. Till you become familiar with this house and the guests are around, you can take help of servants, or even me, to make yourself comfortable.' Naina said this so kindly that Suman did not feel even for a minute that she was not at her own house.

A new house, new surroundings, but Suman felt as comfortable as she was in her own house. Kunal was showing Suman the family album, and Naina came in to join them. And then she placed two air tickets in Kunal's hand saying,

'Your honeymoon tickets to Goa. Your father and I always loved this place, so I planned your trip without asking you. I hope you will like the place. And Kunal, take very good care of my daughter, not daughter-in-law,' looking at Suman she said.

Suman felt overwhelmed with Naina's affection. She thought of telling Kunal that instead of the honeymoon they should stay with his family for a few more days, but Kunal was already thanking his mother for the tickets, and she remained silent, smiling.

Before they left for the airport, Naina called Suman to the prayer room. She asked Suman to spread and hold the corners of her dupatta with her two hands; the way one would ask for blessings before god. Naina had put a streak of vermillion in between Suman's hair parting. She started putting turmeric coloured rice and some money in Suman's dupatta and spoke, 'Suman this tradition of filling the anchal with turmeric colored grains and money symbolizes that the women is the store of prosperity and happiness of a family. It will be you who will be responsible to convert your house into a heaven. It is you who will fill my son's life with happiness and I have full faith in you that you can do this.' With her token items and words of blessings, Naina had imparted the whole philosophy of life to Suman. Suman folded the dupatta with her blessings, and wished that her life stays simple, always.

It was an enchanting beginning to her new life...

After the announcement for security check the couple waved goodbye to their relatives. The flight took off, and Suman was in her world of dreams. In the flight packed with people, with sound of bells to beckon stewardesses, to and fro running around of flight crew—there was only one sound audible to Suman and Kunal, and that was the beat of their hearts.

The booking agent had taken care to book one of the best hotel rooms for them. Even amongst honeymoon suites, the room was the best located. It was the corner most room of the five-star hotel, facing the sea shore and it allowed a beautiful view of sunrise and sunset. The unrestricted and panoramic view of the blue Arabian Sea, the Aguada Fort across the Mandovi river, the absence of a crazy crowd provided the calmness and quietness they wanted.

After a bath, they went to the hotel restaurant for dinner to relish traditional Goan cuisine and Feni. Instead of moving to the hotel room the two decided to take a stroll, barefoot, on the soft and silvery sand bed of the beach, outside their hotel. The lovely beach sparkled in the moonlight to welcome the new couple.

They paddled all along the sea coast and finally sat on a rock where the splashing sea would throw its waves to produce sounds of many tiny bells. The sand engulfed the water in its arms like lovers embracing each other; the sand bed girdled the water and allowed the waves to move only till a particular distance. The sea water, like a disciplined student, followed the rule of high and low tide. The waves coughed up all the debris that it had collected in the prior surge. Once the waves receded the sea stood calm for a while, which made it difficult to imagine the potential it had to cause immense damage, if it got into its murderous frenzy. Suman loved her first experience of the sea coast.

The two of them were gazing at the sea. A wave splashed with force against the rock and left them soaking. Water dripped from Suman, her kurta looked transparent, and it clung to her body; it revealed every bit of her skin beneath her transparent dress in the light of the full moon. Her fair skin glowed with the freshness of youth. The dress defined her body contours. Kunal could not move his eyes away from Suman. He went near her and licked the water drops on her cheeks. Suman gave her approval by moving yet closer to him. His firm body made her go wild. Kunal placed his lips on hers for a passionate kiss and they remained together with their lips interlocked for minutes. Back in the hotel room, Kunal was impatient to satisfy his mounting desire of making love to his wife, but he did not want to cause any trouble to Suman, assuming her to be tired of the ceremonies, and then the journey. Suman, on the other hand, wished Kunal to pick her up in his arms into his tough clasp.

She pulled the curtains close so no light could enter the room. The room was illuminated only with the foyer night lamp. They both lay in bed and looked at each other. Suman and Kunal tried to gauge the extent of tiredness from each other's face. Getting sleep was becoming a far cry. It had deserted both, and cupid, the love god, had taken charge. Their hot breath did all the talking. It spoke everything without the aid of either the eyes or lips.

Kunal came near Suman and placed his hand on her heart.He could feel the beat saying something. He pressed his hand closer to feel her skin. Suman aided him by unfastening the knots of her night gown to make way for Kunal's hand which rested on her soft breasts. He could feel her heightening heartbeat and he held her tightly in his clasp. She could feel the intense heat from the kisses he planted all over her body; the heat of his touch, his lips and between his legs. His desire matched her cravings.

The boundaries were crossed and the two bodies came close and lost identity to become one—like the earth meeting the sky at the horizon. Suman could feel Kunal throbbing deep within her. Though there would be many such private moments in their life but the excitement of the first sexual rendezvous transcended all earthly experiences. The honeymoon got over almost in no time. Suman and

Kunal had to come back to join their offices, and to get back to their normal routine.

Kunal was still in bed enjoying his sleep. Suman had woken up early that day to savour the beauty of the early morning sunrise. She turned her head to look at Kunal, sleeping as relaxed as a baby sleeping in the lap of his mother. The bright rays of the sun were hitting her making her feel their warmth. She remembered the warmth she felt sipping a hot cup of tea debating the latest political and economic issues with her parents and siblings.

Her mother hardly participated in any discussion, but she was forced to be a part of the discussion just for her smiles and chides and to stop the debate getting hot. How Mom's presence energized them to do things, and it would bring a smile on her face. That one smile kept them charged the whole day for directing their efforts in the right direction.

She was all by herself. As per her old habit, she got into retrospection of her changing life. Suman missed her mother a lot and she immediately pressed the buttons on her mobile to call up her mother and listen to her voice. After talking for a while her mother said that there were enquiries from her office and the office people wanted her to join back as early as possible. She realized that she had got her leave extended twice on phone without any formal approval by the authorities.

Though Suman felt better after talking to her mother,

she was surrounded with the blues of being back to office. She had still not gotten over Rajan's memories, and now it would be difficult for her to work in the same office without Rajan, and even if Rajan came back, her life would become all the more complicated, she thought.

She thought of sharing Rajan's story with Kunal, but there was a risk of spoiling her married life. She had stored those memories in some remote corner of her heart.

Her thoughts were in turmoil when she heard Kunal's voice calling her, 'Suman, where are you?'

Suman came in from the balcony to the room where Kunal was reclining on the sofa, sipping his tea with the morning newspaper in front of him. His eyes swiftly moved from one end of the page to another, trying to devour knowledge and to catch up with the happenings in and around the world.

Without looking at her, he spoke,'Suman, I am about to finish my second cup of tea and where were you?'

'Just relishing nature's beauty,' Suman said with a smile.

Kunal showed his concern and said, 'Why don't you order tea for yourself. I have finished the entire pot!' He put his legs down from the sofa and poured the leftover tea into his cup.

Suman came and sat next to Kunal and called up room service for her hot cup of tea. Kunal was flipping through the newspaper reading aloud the important headlines to Suman and then he got stuck on a piece of news, 'A thirteen-year-old child from an elite school commits suicide. He was suffering from depression.'

Suman asked, 'But why should a child, who should be bubbly and lively, suffer from depression?'

'Hmm! Reason! Who has time to find the reason? Both parents of this child are successful professionals; both of them had no time to spend with their child and know about his feelings, apprehensions or answer his queries! Who would have answered them—maids or nannies?The smart and intelligent parents had assured that the child had the latest gizmos. He was attending an elite school; he had the best tutors who could be hired. For them, these were the requirements for a child that made him enjoy life, and made him happy and successful. They forgot that their child needed investment of parents' time, love and care for his overall well-being as an individual.'

He folded the newspaper and placed it on the table. 'Oh! It is so sad to read such news.' The pain was reflected deep in his eyes. 'I don't understand where will our desire for money, fame and status take us? Why do parents think of bringing a life in this world if they have no time for the children? Imagine, we even forget why we need such material things—for our children, or for ourselves?'

'Anyway,' Kunal got off his seat and moved near his luggage telling Suman, "We shall be checking out by 11am, please get ready by that time. I am almost through with my packing, only the gifts we have bought for everyone remain to be packed.'

'Do not worry; I shall be packing them. But first of all, let me make a phone call to my office to know why they had called up Mom.'

'Maybe they want you to join urgently. In that case we would have the added work of sorting out our belongings and get your ticket preponed to Delhi.'

The plan was for Suman to accompany Kunal to Mumbai, and leave for Delhi after staying for two days, to pursue her application for her transfer to Mumbai.

Suman smiled and made a call to her Delhi office.To her pleasant surprise, she was transferred to Mumbai and she was to join the Mumbai office directly after her leave.

Working at the Delhi office would have been difficult because of the trail of memories of her days with Rajan; also, she did not want to stay away from Kunal.

TWENTY-THREE

SUMAN ROSE UP early in the morning to prepare the breakfast and tiffin—both Kunal's and hers. All the things his mother used to do, she had to do now.

Back from office, she felt too tired to cook so she ordered a take-away. Suman had laid the table feeling guilty serving Kunal the restaurant food because her mom-in-law, Naina, had specifically told her that Kunal liked home cooked food. He had a servant who cooked for him or he just had milk and fruit for his dinner.

Kunal made a pretence of liking the food because he knew that asking Suman to cook after coming back from office was expecting too much from her. But he also realized that he could not have carried on like this for a long time. He arranged for a full time help to manage their household.

The initial few days passed smoothly, though Suman hardly had time to spend with Kunal. Despite sitting in her cushy office making negotiations for the best deal for her company, she felt a vacuum being created in her life. It was back to the same old routine as both of them were getting loaded with more and more work from their office. Life was becoming mechanical, and she felt her life was like a programmed machine with a set pattern of activities to perform.

"Was earning money her aim, or did she wish to climb the corporate ladder with designations going from big to bigger? Then, what shall make me happy?" She asked herself the question.

She was clear about one thing that she did not like being bound in shackles of restraints on her time, or of not being able to do what she wanted. And one day, while driving back from office, she took a decision. She would quit her job to have control over her time. To do something that made her happy. Suman was happy with herself because she could take a decision for her own life. She felt she was in full control of her life. "But this freedom over time will be at the cost of losing my financial independence! How can I lose my financial freedom?" she thought. But cheques with additional zeros being added to it every passing year might cost her the pleasure of her family life.

With the big question looming in her mind she was at the crossroads of choosing between her family life and her career! She had to choose; she could not just have her cake and eat it too! She thought that it would take her time to understand her husband and her household so as to be at the helm of affairs. To strengthen her family, she needed to nurture its roots so that it blossomed into happiness. No one could undermine the importance of money, but it had its limitations; it could not buy many things which made life complete and worth living.

She decided that she would let her career bear the brunt to make her family life happy. Her husband was in a position to look after the family's financial needs.

She realized that she loved her mother the most, and may be, that was the reason she wanted to become like her—someone who did not mind losing her identity to become the foundation of strength and the fountain of love for her family. With her relentless service and undivided attention to her family she had made the world an oyster for her children and a bulwark for her husband to climb the success ladder. Her promotion was when father had a promotion or when she or her siblings excelled in studies and sports. Her reward was just a 'thank you' from them saying that she was the best mother or the best wife. How could she deprive her children of the privileges her mother gave to them?

Suman was feeling lighter after taking a decision. Without focusing on what she was losing she rejoiced thinking of what she would be gaining. Her heart was full of joy, and when Kunal came back she broke the news at the dinner table.

'Kunal, what if you find me waiting for you, every day, with hot and delicious food cooked by me?'

'What do you mean? Are you changing your job to a hotel? I mean, I really can't understand what you are saying!'

'Kunal I will not be going to the office now because I want to quit working.' Suman said.

'What..!' Kunal was shocked when Suman dropped the bombshell!

'Quit working! You've gone nuts sweety! People are dying to get a job, and you are talking of giving up your excellent career for no rhyme or reason. Who spurns such a lucrative career?'

'I will,' said Suman in clear cogent words. 'Kunal, have you realized that our life is getting stuck in a rut. We have no time for each other. And we are becoming like cogs of a machine to mint money, for what? Are you not earning enough to make a comfortable living for us?'

Suman had a valid point. Kunal too became thoughtful after listening to her. But still he wanted her to be fully assured. 'Are you sure? I don't want to hear complaints later that your marriage cost you your independence!'

'No darling! I have thought about it well. And since I have taken a decision, I will not step back from fulfilling what I have decided!'

Kunal happily said, 'Ok Madam! I salute your decision.' Suman was happy to get Kunal's support.

TWENTY-FOUR

SHE WENT TO HER office with the resignation letter; there were questions, advice and suggestions at every desk. But hers was a well thought out decision. Despite her colleagues' suggestion that quitting a promising career could be the big mistake of her life, she did not deter and stuck to her guns.

She left the office amidst scoffs, surprises and sneers dominating the topic of the office gossip column and finding its way in the whispers of the junior staff. Faces veneered with forced smiles bade her adieu wishing her well for her life. While giving her resignation letter she had wiped off even the minimal connection she had with the past.

After resigning her job, Suman had all her time for herself. She had her small unit, her household under her charge. She was a one-man army, her own boss, to plan and decide how to spend her time, to plan her budget, the daily menu etc. She was the chef, marketing manager, finance manager and the CEO, a single person with all the power vested in her.

She would wake up in the morning to the sound of the doorbell buzzing like an alarm clock announcing the arrival of the milkman and the newspaper. A to-do list was planned, jotted down and pinned on the board outside her kitchen. She set her important targets to meet for that day, like shopping for a new item, or trying a new recipe, or visiting a nearby ATM to draw cash, or collect the form to apply for IPO of a blue-chip company that she analyzed as having good growth and earning potential.

She was enjoying fixing her targets and meeting her own deadlines; her objective being a happy home of people with smiling faces. She was enjoying every bit of her home life.

Kunal happily concentrated on his work. He looked forward to variety on the breakfast table before leaving for office. The new dishes in his tiffin made his colleagues look for a reason to have lunch with him. When he compared these days to his bachelor days he could understand why his mother always insisted on getting him married to a sweet and loving girl.

He remembered his bachelor days—how he used to wake up lazily and rush to office, at times on an empty stomach, or gorging on a piece of bread with some butter picked up hurriedly, because he did not have time to even toast his bread. He mainly relied on canteen food and the awful tasting food cooked by the cook who came in just to cook the dinner. From the time Suman joined him he felt more energetic. He did not get exhausted the way he did earlier. He looked forward to reaching home early because he knew she would be ready with a delicious snack for him in his beautiful house. What more could a person ask for in life? he wondered, 'Is this kind of happiness an epitome of heaven?'

He would, at times, thank Suman for her decision to stay back at home. He had started enjoying the pampering of his wife.

Suman, on the other hand, went that extra mile to beautify her house with various hues of happiness; the spic and span house, aroma of delicious food cooked with love, and dreams of happiness for her family. She had been gathering pieces of information about setting up her kitchen from various sources; calling up her mother to magazines—to any valid source she could lay her hands on. She now had a kitchen with all modern gadgets but with a traditional tinge.

The mason jars had all varieties of pickles—from

cauliflower-carrot, raw mango to lemon and chilies—all home made. During weekends, Kunal and Suman would spend the entire day together, watching movies, gossiping, or talking about their families etc. And then the backups came handy; to cook something quick and serve with the mouth-watering accompaniments to make the holiday enjoyable in each other's company.

The main perk she enjoyed due to her stay at home was the afternoon siesta, which was never possible while working in the office.

And one day Suman thought, "I will not sleep in the afternoon today." She had decided to try a new Thai recipe that she had seen in the new monthly women's magazine. Suman had very little kitchen experience before marriage. She had always thought kitchen work was the most mundane work because her mother was looking after her and the complete household, never letting her be in the kitchen so that she could concentrate on her studies. At times, Mom was short on time to even sit and chat with them, and then she used to join her Mom in the kitchen telling her, 'Mom you get hyper about everything. Can't you leave your work for tomorrow.'

Her mother said, 'Suman I cannot let work pile up for tomorrow,' and then she would start mentioning her 'to do' list for the next day.

Suman could now put herself in her mother's shoes. With tears in her eyes she said, 'Thanks Mom'.

Suman hardly knew anything about cooking, except some recipes she had learnt in cooking classes that she attended during her vacations, when she was in her high school. Those recipes came in handy to serve food for first few days. Thereafter, she called up her mother or mother-in-law to learn a few recipes that Kunal relished. But just by writing the recipes she was not able to get the taste perfectly. Suman would keep working on samples to finally get the taste she wanted.

'The way to a man's heart is through his stomach'—this piece of knowledge was shared by an old lady who advocated the importance of cooking to young girls. The old lady ran a small tiffin business supplying tiffins in offices. The household ladies ordered the tiffins whenever they were under the weather and could not cook.

At times, the old lady would visit houses to spend her free time, where she was welcomed by the ladies as she always lifted their sagging morale with her anecdotes which highlighted the importance of a woman in making the family structure strong. Young girls sometimes told her, 'Dadi Amma, keep this advice for your countryside girls whose only option in life is to be a housewife.' They always ridiculed her.

How rightly she replied, 'If all of you are busy in just earning money, then who will take care of our future generation? What will happen to our culture and civilization? We will have an uncivilized society imitating the traits of the maids; what values can you expect a maid to teach a child?'

'Then why should we waste our time and effort in studying? We should instead enjoy our life without bothering to study!'

And the answer given by the old lady gave food for thought. She said, 'Why do you girls or rather everyone think that the purpose of education is just to earn money? Why don't you understand that the purpose of education is to make you lead a happy life, which is by being bold enough to take decisions in the light of knowledge? The purpose of education is to make a better society for us and for our future generations. An educated mother can raise sensible and responsible children who are mentally and emotionally strong. Education gives you the strength to be self-reliant, and if at all there is a crisis in life and it becomes a necessity, then you can use your knowledge to earn money.' The talks of the old lady seemed quite relevant to Suman. She had lot of time to retrospect while being busy in her work.

After taking her bath, Suman picked up the new issue of the women's magazine, and turned the pages to the recipe that she had decided to cook.

She called up her nearby grocery store from where she ordered her monthly groceries to send her the ingredients. 'At the earliest the items will reach you in an hour's time,'the sales person attending her call told her. She thought of finishing some preparations before the delivery boy arrived with shrimps and basil for the Red Curry Shrimps.

But just after a few moments, the doorbell started ringing. Suman wondered how the order could reach so soon? She looked at the time and it was just five minutes before that she had placed her order. She rushed to open the door and decided to give a piece of her mind to the person whom she assumed to be someone promoting some product for some company.

She was murmuring, "The marketing stunts are just to trouble people. The sales guys and girls just barge into houses, whenever they feel like. And what has happened to the security? Are they sleeping?" She turned the door handle with her right hand, and with the other hand she slid the bolt fixed at the top of the door down,her face red with agitation.

But the moment the face of the person standing at the door became visible, her expression changed. 'You...now, at this hour...so early!'

Her mouth was open wide with amazement!

'I mean you never come back at this time!' It was Kunal back from office before his usual time.

Kunal looked amused and said, 'Suman you look so startled to have me at this time as if you were waiting for someone else.' Kunal pulled Suman's leg.

'Kunal stop it! You can think whatever you wish to! It is for you to trust me or not, I don't need to give you explanations unnecessarily.'

Suman was angry, but Kunal was in a very good mood and he very well knew how to placate his lovely wife. He held Suman in a tight embrace saying, 'Darling, I love you, and you don't owe me any explanation.'

He unleashed his passion by kissing her on the lips; their lips were interlocked for a while and then suddenly Suman pushed Kunal back.

'What happened?' Kunal asked.

'Kunal let me turn off the gas. I can smell my spices burning.' She rushed towards the kitchen and spoke loudly, 'Kunal you go and change, and I shall get tea for you. And I also have a surprise dish for dinner.'

Instead of going to his room, Kunal followed Suman to the kitchen, He clasped her in his strong arms from behind her and said, 'Even I have a surprise for you; postpone your cooking for some other day, we are going out for dinner.'

'Why, are you bored of my cooking?' Suman asked.

'No, I want my beautiful wife to take care of me in the same way as she is doing now. Suman, I have got a letter of appreciation for my excellent performance and an increment too given exclusively to me.' He placed a letter in Suman's hand and added, 'This is much before our annual assessment, and during annual assessment I shall be getting the promotion.'

Suman was very excited. She had never felt so happy before, not even when she got her own promotion.

Suman dressed up to suit the mood of the day; the black body fitting gown that Kunal bought her during their honeymoon, a light make-up, and her long hair forming a knot, with strands of loose hair pinned up. Some wisps still managed to escape and casually rested around her pink cheeks. The long diamond earrings sparkled with the matching diamond pendant in the necklace. She looked unusually pretty in the attire, which contrasted with her very fair complexion. Kunal too looked dashing in his casuals.

Kunal took Suman to a disco bar. The DJ played disco hits and the couples danced on the dance floor shaking their bodies vigorously. The music kept changing in the background; hip hop, rock and salsa. And the elaborate colourful lighting throbbed to the beat of the music. The couples in their frenzied dancing mood reached the guests sitting and enjoying their drinks. Some yielded to their request to join them on the floor, while others gently denied the overture.

Suman and Kunal enjoyed their drinks and the music.

Kunal stole those moments to have a look at his beautiful wife, who was too engrossed in watching the couples dancing. His eyes rested on her face illuminated by the changing colors of the disco lights. Suman was getting lost in the beats and unconsciously her feet tapped and fingers stroked the glass in her hand. She was not aware that Kunal was watching her so closely.

Kunal's eyes savoured every inch of Suman from head to toe. The touch of kohl in her eyes enhanced their depth. Kunal gazed at her eyes, their temptation could make many young hearts die the death of 'Jatinga' he thought. He could now understand the famous 'Jatinga' story of north-eastern India, where many birds have sacrificed their lives on the altar of love light.(*Jatinga, famous for the phenomenon of birds "committing suicide", is located on a spur of the Haflong ridge, the headquarter of the district. The mist and fog covers the area like a veil around the beautiful face of a damsel from September to November. During these late monsoon months, the mysterious behaviour of birds takes place.*)

The fine contours of her lips trembled and moved with the lyrics of the songs. Kunal was losing his control and it was difficult for him to wait. He wished to have solitude to savour the company of only his wife to dive deep in the sea of love. And he hurried with their dinner to reach back home.

The dark veil of night engulfed tired souls in its arms

for a restful sleep. Only two pulsating hearts were awake; the love god empowered them with its blessings.

Kunal kissed Suman on her breasts, on her neck, ears and her hand. He forced her gown to slip off, removed her hairpins, and moved his hand all over to feel the soft, silky touch of her body. His senses were gratified; he was marvelling at the gorgeousness of the beautiful body of his wife. Suman's yearnings grew with each word of love that Kunal murmured in her ears. They made love, till their craving mounted and Suman could feel Kunal deep within her. His heat, his body fragrance all got ingrained within her. Their bodies merged into an eternal embrace to realize the ecstasy of union of soul, mind, heart. Every inch of her skin and flesh had the mark of Kunal; his touch, his smell and his love. Suman savored the moments of love with her eyes closed.

Their love was permanently implanted within Suman. It was the beginning of physical discomfort, but her heart swelled with beautiful feelings and pleasant dreams for the future.

Kunal started taking extra care of her. The motherhood package consisted of regular visits to the doctor for monitoring the child's development and to seek solutions for the symptoms like nausea, heart burns, morning sickness and all such small things that can make a person uncomfortable.

Motherhood, which every woman craves to experience at least once in her life, gives the heavenly feeling of being a creator to a woman. The embodiment of love between two persons is given an added binding to strengthen their relationship. The ground was being readied for the arrival of a new soul with lots of enthusiasm.

TWENTY-FIVE

IT WAS ONE of the most important days in Suman's life when she held her little angel in her arms. Kunal named his daughter Kusum, meaning 'flower'. Suman kept gazing at her soft face, her tightly closed eyes and her spontaneous smiles and cries. Kusum was the personification of her love for Kunal. And the child meant a responsibility for both of them. But Suman was happy and made a resolution in her mind, 'I shall raise my child in the best possible manner.'

The baby's cry diverted her attention. She rocked her in her arms, kissed her, but when the child continued to cry she put her in the cradle, and started looking around for someone to help her. She was becoming fidgety, running to and fro in the room, making an effort to look for something to stop her child from crying. But Kusum's cries became yet louder. Suman's confidence got all shaky. And then her gaze fell on the bell switch next to her bed and she pressed the bell to call a nurse to help her. "Well, it is a tough task to deal with a newborn baby. How will I handle her all alone?" She thought.

The nurse arrived, and lifted the baby. She told Suman to give her feed. 'The baby is hungry.' She made Suman sit on the hospital bed with the back support and put Kusum near Suman's chest and bared one breast. With closed eyes, the baby could identify the touch of the nipple, held it with her lips, and started sucking the milk.

The middle-aged nurse was talking aloud, 'A baby builds connection with the world through its whimpers. She has to satisfy her hunger. And nature maintains a baby's food supply of milk through mother's breasts.'

Suman appeared worried! 'How will I take care of her all alone? How will I understand what the baby needs?' The nurse said, 'Well, I can't say how people in the west take care of their little ones without the support of families, but here, in India, we have to rely on experienced ladies in the family. Don't you have any elderly lady? I mean, your mother or mom-in-law!'.

'I am fortunate to have them both, but circumstances are such that they cannot join me at present. My mom-in-law can't move from her station because she has had a stroke recently; she has been advised to take bed rest for a few months, and my mother has moved with my father to his posting in Africa, where he cannot be left alone as he is suffering from severe diabetes, and there is dearth of medical facilities.'

'Then you should have gone to your mother-in-law's place,' said the nurse.

'But medical facilities in smaller towns are just not adequate,' replied Suman.

By that time Kunal was back. He overheard part of Suman's conversation with the nurse. He sat beside Suman and asked the nurse 'Sister, do you feel I am not taking good care of my wife and daughter?'

'I don't mean that, Sir. You seem to be a very caring and affectionate husband, but the presence of an experienced lady always helps.'

'Anyway, Ma'am, you don't need to worry because nature is there for assistance, to be the practical guide, in the form of intuition of a mother.'

TWENTY-SIX

SUMAN TOOK UP the challenge and enjoyed every moment of it. The days changed to months and months into years; time flew as if with wings. And life changed for Suman, as quickly as flipping the pages of a book. Kusum changed from an infant to a toddler, and then to an age to attend kindergarten.

'Kusum...Kusum', the sound followed the dancing and prancing Kusum from one sofa chair to another, from kitchen to the bathroom. From the bathroom to the bedroom and to every corner of the house, wherever she went, Suman followed her like a shadow to get her ready for school. Kusum's capering around the house made Suman's task difficult. Finally, she caught hold of her, made her sit in her lap, and got her dressed before the school van came.

Once dressed and in the van, Kusum looked happy to be with kids of her own age. The cherubic child blew kisses to her mom with her cute chubby hand. And Suman sighed with relief, nodding her head and reciprocating her darling's gesture as she walked back to her house.

After Kusum left for school, Suman did not know how to spend her time. She was not able to take prudent time management decisions. For years now, she had gotten into the habit of catering to her over packed schedule. The activities were lined up, one after another, and everything pivoted around Kusum, or Kunal. There was no time for herself. Kunal and Kusum blocked all her time so that she would rush through even her daily routine chores. Her life had become so mechanical that she had forgotten how else the time could be used.

And then she remembered how she had relished devouring the dailies with a hot cup of tea, or just chatting with mom, dad and her siblings.

She put on the radio and started humming the lyrics of the song being played as she brewed some tea. While readying the tea, her mind drifted to Kusum. "How will she settle in the school? What shall I prepare for dinner?"

Then she smiled and chided herself, "Old habits die hard. Can't I put aside my routine and relish a cup of tea? If I don't plan and finish my work fast, it will be time for

Kusum to come back from school. I have to go and pick her up from the stop as well."

The tea was ready, and snapping out of her thoughts she was seated with her hot cup of cardamom tea with the newspaper spread in front of her. A few sips from her cup, and she was through with the headlines. And then she turned the pages to have a look at page 3, but her open hair flew all over her face and caused a lot of disturbance in reading the newspaper. It was being difficult to control her hair going haywire. So, she placed her cup and thought of tying her hair in a knot. She ran her fingers down the hair length to straighten its entanglement, but the fingers moved through the hair strands collecting a bunch of broken hair with them.

She used both her hands at the back of her head to catch the hair and rotated it to form a loop; the hair had stopped drifting on her face, but she had almost a bunch of hair left in her hand.

"Oh my god! Look at my hair, what's going wrong with it. With this spate of hair fall, I am not very far from getting bald. I must start caring for my hair," she murmured.

She was sitting in front of the mirror to massage and comb her hair. Mechanically her mind started playing records from her past days. Her long, silky hair had reigned supreme as the topic of discussion amongst her friends. A few even suggested that she should try her luck at modelling for hair product ads. And mom's Saturday night hot oil hair massage, followed by washing the hair the next day. But all this sounded like luxury now. For all the years, since Kusum's birth, where was the time for beautification? She had to rush through all her work, to the extent of even cutting down on her sleep!

With endless daily chores, and a darling little baby who was vulnerable if left alone, Suman could not think of relaxing as long as Kusum was awake. Then, when Kusum slept, she finished her household tasks. Suman had enjoyed every bit of raising Kusum all alone; from singing lullabies to playing peek-a-boo, from taking her to the paedritician for routine vaccinations or minor ailments, following her like a shadow, day in and day out—every time and everywhere.

Kunal was another recipient of household services. His contribution was to bring the money home, and Suman looked after everything else. Suman had efficiently divided the household responsibilities into outside house and within house. She ensured her home was a powerhouse for recharging the exhausted energy. For Kunal to wake up fresh and energetic, she spent sleepless nights with Kusum in a different room to ensure he had undisturbed sleep. In the list of her priorities, she had always ranked her needs as last. The time available had two principal slots—first for Kusum, then for Kunal, and the smallest slot was for her. She got up from the dressing stool, and walked a few steps towards the mirror. On reaching closer, she fixed her glance on her image, wishing that the mirror, at least, would show her traces of her past. And when her eyes refused to recognize her as the Suman she knew, she was almost on the verge of tears. She said in disgust, "No, it is not possible! How can I look so bad?" She adjusted the light from the window, wiped the mirror using her hand, "may be something is wrong with the mirror."

But nothing changed and she appeared very much like before. Her heart wailed at her appearance!

The dark circles around her eyes narrated the starvation of sleep for days together. Her dull skin complained of lack of attention, and the layers around the midriff had grown by quite a few inches to make her look fat and flabby. It clearly depicted her irregular food habits, basically gorging on the leftovers after feeding her husband and daughter. Her glamorous and attractive looks had changed. Suman came closer to the mirror to look closely at herself, and it further revealed the surface lines and spots that had started to develop on her face.

"In looking after my family, I have ignored myself." Negative thoughts started clouding her mind, but then the enlightenment of higher philosophy in her subconscious mind restored her lost morale.

"But I am not a selfish mother, or a selfish wife."

"Kunal does not love me for how I look. We are soulmates, and we know how to appreciate each other's souls. I am so stupid to think like a teenager. Ours is not an infatuation that will change like the changing seasons."

She stood before the mirror for some time, and picked up the bottle of hair oil. As soon as she tilted the bottle to pour some oil to massage, the phone rang. She poured the oil back in the bottle, and rushed to take the call.

Kunal spoke from the other end, 'Where were you, Suman? How long do you take to pick up the phone? Anyway, you and Kusum be ready in the evening because you have to come with me for my office party.'

'What party K.....?' Kunal had banged the phone without even listening to what Suman had to ask!

"Why is he so rude? He must be in the middle of some meeting." Suman thought giving the benefit of the doubt to her husband.

"But, he wants Kusum to come with us to the party!" she thought. Since Kusum's birth, Suman had stopped going to the parties because it was against the party norm to attend it with kids. Suman was never in favor of hiring and leaving her daughter in the custody of a nanny and attending late night parties.

"Well," she said to herself, "let me stop presuming and

wait for Kunal to come and tell me everything." No oiling of hair even today!

She put the cap back on the bottle and moved towards her wardrobe to look for a decent party dress. She ransacked it from top to bottom. But she had outgrown all her dresses. When it came to saris, she could not fit into any of her old blouses.

There was only one salwar-kameez coming to the rescue; the one she would never have worn if she had a better choice. The baby pink brocade was too flashy to be worn for formal gatherings. This dress, which she had worn on her first Diwali after marriage, was stitched bigger in size, to fit her at that time when she was expecting Kusum. Suman had no other choice, other than this only available dress.

Had Kunal told her even a day earlier about the party, she could have easily bought a new dress. And then her long overdue shopping too would have been possible. Suman was feeling slightly offended.

"But, it is quite possible that it is a surprise party!"

Suman's mind kept getting enmeshed with her own logics and explanations, and Kunal entered the house. It was much earlier than the other days.

His face bore a lovely smile, but it was not for her. His countenance changed looking at Suman, 'Suman, both of you get ready fast,' he commanded.

Suman asked in a low tone, 'What is this surprise party for and that too with the family?'

'Suman, can you stop conjecturing? For your information, it is not a surprise party! It was planned a fortnight ago to celebrate our company's success and to felicitate departmental heads who brought all credit to the company.'

Suman said, 'Congrats Kunal!' The news of Kunal's promotion made her feel on top of the world; she felt that her efforts were being rewarded, but at the same time the dress situation had her troubled. Her face was gloomy.

'Kunal, but why did you not tell me about the party earlier?' This time she had raised her voice a bit.

Kunal stared at her and said in a raised tone, 'Will you stop acting like a typical nag? I don't owe you any explanation! Had it not been mandatory, I would have preferred to go to the party all alone.'

She too felt annoyed and said, 'Kunal I am asking you, why didn't you tell me about the party before?'

Without answering her question he asked her 'Why, what happened? Did I not call you up to get ready for the party?'

'I don't mean today. When you knew that there was going to be a party, you should have told me about it! Had I known earlier, at least I could have made preparations to look presentable. I don't have a dress to wear today!'

'Oh, come on Suman! You have your wardrobe full of dresses, and you are saying you have nothing to wear. Just pull out any damn dress because whatever you wear you'll look the same. Please, don't have a very high opinion of yourself. People will see you as my wife and not the dress you wear. And, fashion suits people who keep themselves fit.'

Kunal's statement was sarcastic. His words were as sharp as a rapier and it wounded her badly. She was no more as happy as she was a moment ago. The arrogance in his voice had masked Kunal, whom she loved. It was not a husband talking to his wife; it was the chief snubbing a subordinate. Suman felt reluctant to accompany him for the party but she did not say so. At that moment, it would have meant spoiling for a fight.

TWENTY-SEVEN

KUNAL LOOKED UNUSUALLY handsome in his cream colored summer suit with a teal tie. He had always been particular about maintaining his wardrobe as per the latest fashion. Suman walked behind Kunal holding Kusum in her arms as she refused to walk on her own. Suman expected Kunal to render a helping hand, to at least carry Kusum, his loving daughter, but he looked too engrossed in his thoughts—too busy to take notice of his family.

Suman, sad and despondent, followed Kunal to the party lawn, full of office staff and their families. Everyone had glasses filled with drinks in their hand—sipping juice, wine or a cocktail, along with appetizing snacks. For Suman and Kusum, it was a crowd of unfamiliar people. Carrying Kusum in her arms, she waited behind Kunal wherever he halted to talk or for a handshake. She too mechanically responded to the greetings or courtesy extended to her as Kunal's spouse.

The bartenders of a reputed five-star hotel criss-crossed before the guests, and served snacks and drinks. Suman became busy with the waiter carrying chicken tikka and then moved near an attendant holding a soft drink tray. She picked up a glass of apple juice for Kusum. Having picked up food and drink of Kusum's choice she thought of asking Kunal to help her take a seat so that she could feed Kusum. But Kunal had moved on without even bothering to check whether she was comfortable or not! She looked around to spot him amongst the groups of men and ladies busy chatting, but he could not be seen. Maybe he had gone out of the party lawn, she mused. She moved to a round table adorned with a red satin table cloth spread over a white base cloth, topped with a small vase kept in the center of the table with three roses. She sat on a chair and made Kusum sit on the one next to it.

Being in a crowd with unfamiliar faces was altogether a new experience for Kusum. She was becoming uncomfortable. A few teenagers came to sit on the empty chairs around the table where Suman had positioned herself with Kusum. The children tried being friendly with the little child, but Kusum became yet more restless. She jumped in Suman's lap and hid her face on her shoulders to avoid any contact with strangers. The mothers of the children sitting near Suman joined her at the table and began chatting with her.

'What happened to the baby?'

'What do you want, baby?' A beautiful lady asked Kusum in a sweet and melodious voice placing her hand on Kusum's chubby hand. She was wearing a navy-blue Kanjivaram sari with a wide golden border. Her forehead was adorned with a big black bindi and a thick line of red vermillion beautified the center parting of her braided long hair.

She went on to introduce herself to Suman, 'By the way, I am Namita Khanna. My husband's name is JC Khanna. He has been working in this company for the past fifteen years and I know almost every employee and their families, but I am sorry I am not able to figure out whether I have met you earlier or not!'

'My husband's name is Kunal.'

'That's great! You are Kunal's wife!' Mrs Khanna said in an excited tone.

'I have met Kunal so many times! He has even come to our house a few times with my husband. He reports to my husband, but somehow, I never had a chance of meeting you before, not even at the annual employees' meet.'

'Yes ma'am. Because of my small child I prefer to be at home,' said Suman.

'I can understand!' empathizing with Suman Mrs Khanna said.

A few ladies followed Mrs Khanna, one of them carrying a cup of coffee for her. Mrs Khanna introduced Suman to the group of ladies.

'Are you Mrs Kunal?' a lady asked with surprise.

'Why? What happened?' asked Mrs Khanna.

'No, nothing. I saw Kunal enjoying drinks with a lady near the bar, and I thought her to be his wife,' the lady said rotating her eyeballs.

She pointed her finger towards the bar and said, 'Look there!'

Suman looked baffled as all other ladies looked at her sympathetically. Suman felt shattered. Maybe mocking was a better word to describe what they felt for Suman.

She had a dilemma—to smile or not to smile. She excused herself. She said she was going to get some ice-cream to pacify Kusum. Instead of the ice-cream stall, she headed towards the bar where the men and the women were pouring drinks in their glasses. Behind the bar, she could see two figures sitting close to each other; the figure of a man and a woman. On moving closer, she could clearly identify that the man was Kunal.

The woman was wearing a blue-black chiffon strapless gown with sparkling golden sequins. The dress clung to her body to accentuate the curves, and the skin of her shoulders, back, and cleavage was exposed. She had put on heavy make up and embellished herself with diamond jewellery. It made her look extremely sensual.

She was sitting close to Kunal. They both held wine glasses in their hands. The physical proximity was more than enough to suggest the closeness they shared. Kusum had started calling, 'Papa…papa' to attract her father's attention, but Kunal was so absorbed in talking to the lady that he did not notice his daughter calling him. Kusum freed herself from the hold of her mother and rushed towards Kunal.

But Suman's steps were momentarily immobilized, as if her heart forgot to supply blood to her body. She didn't know how to react. The green-eyed monster overpowered the woman in her, like any normal human being. It was difficult for her to pretend to be a modern broad-minded wife, who did not mind the presence of some other woman in her husband's life. She was boiling with anger, but pretended to smile. How difficult it was to handle two contrasting emotions, only Suman could know! And it became too much for her to bear the situation and the fury in her heart changed to tears, ready to cross the boundaries of her beautiful eyes.

Lest anyone notice and begin asking questions, she diverted her attention to her daughter, and followed Kusum with racing steps. 'Kusum, my darling, don't run baby!'

But by that time Kusum had almost reached Kunal, who unwillingly looked towards his wife and daughter. Though he was vexed to see his family disturb his comfort zone with his lady partner, publicly he could not have manifested that he was going wild inside. He extended a forced greeting to them, trying to hide the frown on his face. He said, 'Oh, Suman and Kusum where were you? Come and meet…'

'Tara', the lady spoke and moved near Suman. She spoke her name snootily. Her eyes looked over Suman from head to her toe, and she brought forward her trembling hand for a handshake. The lady, in an inebriated state, was not even able to take a few steps steadily.

Kunal went near the lady to support her and make her stand stable.

'Mrs Kunal', she sneered. And her lips twisted into a smile as if she was ridiculing Suman that she had won over Kunal, her husband.

Kunal interrupted to fill in the blanks, 'Tara is my new secretary—an amazing person and a very efficient worker. In fact, maximum credit of my promotion should go to her for her immense support in my work.'

"Tara", Suman thought, "every other woman is much more amazing that the wife." Suman had expected a gentleman's response from her husband, to introduce Suman to his secretary as the person behind all his success.

These words of Kunal acted as the last straw. Suman's glance was fixed on Kunal's face. Her lips were sealed. She wanted to cry loudly but she couldn't. She wanted to tell the whole world about all those small and big sacrifices she had made for her family! Why should she act as a traditional, so called "good girl" of society who is expected to render services without expecting anything in return? At least due acknowledgement should be given to a person who had relentlessly worked for the family. How could she accept herself being belittled before a stranger, who in Suman's opinion was a cheap lady?

The way the two were behaving was not at all professional. Kunal's eyes were fixed on Tara and he made every effort to please her.

Kusum clasped Kunal's legs with both her hands insisting he pick her up in his arms, but Kunal looked reluctant. He placated her by telling her, 'Kusum you are such a darling child. It is small kids who can't stand on their own and get on their parent's lap. Darling, people will make fun of you that you are acting like a little cry baby.'

Kusum could sense her father's disinclination and she stopped insisting with a sulk on her face.

Suman went near Kunal, held him by his arm and shook him saying, 'What are you telling my child? That people will make fun of her, and they will not make fun of this lady whom you are babying. You can't even see that Kusum is getting disturbed because of your indifference!'

Tara interrupted, 'Kunal why don't you ask your wife to handle your child properly? Of what use is she if she cannot even handle her duties properly!'

Tara's words made Suman go berserk. Maybe it would have been a shade less insulting had Kunal told her what Tara had said to her, but with what authority could that lady say this She could not let herself be demeaned to the extent that she could not even maintain the dignity of her soul. She lost her temper, and lifted her hand to give Tara a smack across her face. Before anyone could realize what had gone wrong, she had already lifted Kusum and made her way towards the exit.

Suman hired a cab, and got into it with Kusum to go back to her house. Tears flowed from her eyes hazing out the vision. She kept wiping them and Kusum clung to Suman's chest, looking at her face and kissing her.

Suman was thinking, "had it not been for my selfless and dedicated service, for all the moral and emotional support during difficult times of his career, the success that he claims to be his alone and due to the support of some stranger may not have been possible at all for Kunal. He could work that hard at office with whole-hearted concentration only because of her who was working equally hard at home, preparing the platform so that he could work with a relaxed mind, enthusiasm and energy."

Kusum had slept. Suman carried her from the cab to the house and laid her on the bed. She too lay close to her and closed her eyes so that she could sleep. But, despite having no rest since morning, it was difficult to get any sleep; it was getting difficult even to remain still with eyes closed.

Her mind was getting trapped in the vicious cycle of negative thoughts. Her invincible world of three people was under threat of invasion. This world was her strength to—live, love and be loved. The trust which was the foundation of her family edifice was under threat by a lady.

To put her anxiety to rest, she walked into the balcony; she was in the company of the stars, the moon, and her loneliness. On the black, wide road, there was hardly any vehicle; the road which was a bypass, always used to be jammed with vehicles, and at night in the wee hours, it seemed like waiting for someone to talk about the greatness of the day—which too, like her, was lonely now. The tears flowed from her eyes, unabated, uncontrolled, trying to wash the deep wound cast on her heart by somebody close to it. It is only the closest ones who can cause the deepest wounds; only Kunal could have given her pain of this magnitude.

She was asking herself a question, "Where did I falter? To my knowledge, I made all sacrifices with no expectation, but that does not mean I should be insulted for my good deeds. And who is this lady Tara? Kunal never mentioned about any lady working with him." She remembered that Kunal had always talked about his day at office, while they had dinner, or even when she was busy doing Kusum's work. But, then she realized that there was a gradual change in his behaviour from the past few months, and she had thought it was due to overload of work in office!

TWENTY-EIGHT

TARA WAS A new appointee in KNC Ltd the company where Kunal worked.

KNC Ltd was undergoing a stage of business expansion. And, as an aid to the process, new facilities were created and new recruitments were made.

Kunal's sincerity and hard work had won him a very senior position at a young age. During the upheaval in the company's systems and structures, he became the choice of the senior management to handle additional responsibility. And Tara was randomly picked as Kunal's assistant from amongst the new appointees.

She did not meet many of the criteria specified for the post. Hers was a back door entry because of her high level contacts. She was a close relative of one of the members of the board of trustees. She had no professional or technical qualification, or even any understanding of computers, which was almost a pre-requisite for the job, but she still got the job. Like everywhere else in our country, the rules are meant for people who lack resources and connections.

But Tara had one very big qualification, with which she could outsmart all her contemporaries. She was quite adept at handling her bosses, especially males. She was an attractive, smart and sexy lady, who also had a knack of appearing sexier with her keen sartorial sense. Her tight fitting outfits left little to the imagination. The padded bra added fullness to her bust line, and deep cleavage dresses had the eyes of all men glued to her. Her dressing could be barely called decent in an office environment. Her make-up made her face sparkle throughout the day; kohl in her eyes and rich shades of lipstick making her lips luscious. Her hair was done in curls and folds, but nicely pinned up; she must have been spending hours dressing up, and this was clearly her priority. At the time she joined, her dressing sense aroused a bit of controversy, but she also became an eye candy for most men, except her own boss, Kunal.

The male employees waited for her in the morning, and as she entered office, their performance dropped, like the sensex drops at the news of an illegal takeover of a blue chip company. She enjoyed most of the men swooning and longing for an extra moment in her company. Most of the ladies envied her.

Though she had raised the mercury level in the barometers of most men, but Kunal remained immune to any such impact.

Despite Tara being his assistant, he handled most of his work alone, because he found it easier to finish the work on his own, or by deputing a person with better capability. He always made her inefficiencies at work known to her. He was a difficult boss, and he expected precision in the work from his juniors. He would not relent for Tara, not even for her irresistible attraction.

Kunal never approved of her dressing sense and her sexy demeanor, but he could not openly object to it as it would have meant putting restrictions on someone's personal life. Since she was reporting to him directly, he did not have much of a choice but to bear her. Kunal had restricted her entry to his room only for getting files, or she used to assist him in handling calls when he was busy in meetings.

For Tara, it was like an insult when somebody was ignoring her attraction and Kunal became a challenge to be won over. She understood fully well that he was not an easy target like other men, who would fall prey to her looks and would easily give in to whatever she wanted from them. Kunal belonged to a different genre of men. A well educated and a handsome young man, he was equally erudite. He was a family man who enjoyed being at home after finishing his office. He was sincere and did not mind putting in extra hours at work, but when it came to recreation, he never went out to clubs and hotels without Suman, until it was essentially a part of his official work.

And Tara decided to smash the barriers of a righteous man. When her physical attraction failed to make an impact, she made use of coquettish behavior to worm her way into Kunal's life.

She made sure of attending to even the smallest of his personal needs; like arranging lunch for him at the proper time, serving him tea and coffee at intervals, and many such nitty gritties, which made him comfortable at work. Kunal gradually started becoming used to her services.

The company decided to launch a new product in the market. And this required lot of groundwork. By that time Tara had learnt the basics of computers, and could handle part of the work involving the use of a computer. She assisted Kunal in handling the workload.

When only a week remained for the product to get launched, Kunal even lost track of time to go back home. But, he did not bother his staff much for the work. Most of the burden he handled on his own. He had been particularly concerned about the female staff due to their safety issues.

If at all he needed some person to work overtime, he chose only the male staff.

He needed a week to tie the loose ends before the product launch and for this he preferred to work alone, when most people had left office. One such day, he was working on the press release draft to be sent to the press before the launch. He pressed his bell to call the peon, Sitaram. Whenever he worked till late in the office, it was Sitaram who had to wait. The peon was the last one to leave the office.

Instead of Sitaram, Tara came in and asked, 'What do you want, Sir?'

'Ms Tara, you are still here! Where is Sitaram? Why did he not come?' asked Kunal.

'How many questions will you ask me at one time?' Tara said with a smile on her face with her long eyelashes fluttering. She tried to become friendly with Kunal. 'Shall I answer your queries one by one?'

Kunal nodded with a smile, 'Yeah sure!'

'I have sent Sitaram to get some papers Xeroxed because our machine is not working. Since you are still working, I cannot leave before you, because I am your assistant. Do you want anything. Can I help?' Tara answered Kunal's questions one by one in the order he had asked them.

Kunal appreciated her reply and offered her a seat. 'But I wonder why you are waiting? Don't you know that I am not in favor of ladies working overtime at office. I mean, already ladies who take up employment have to handle double the work pressure at home and office, both. And then there is the safety risk for women. I think you should leave now.'

'Thanks for your concern, but how can I leave when you are still working? When you can work more than the scheduled time, and when we both are being paid for our work then why should only you bear all the pressure,' Tara said.

'Well, you have logic Ms Tara,' Kunal said and smiled.

Tara smiled and posed her question again, 'May I know what you wanted from Sitaram?'

'Yes...yes, I wanted a cup of coffee, because I would need to work for an hour more.'

'Fine sir, can I make coffee for you.'

'You!' asked Kunal surprised, 'But you are not supposed to make coffee for me. That's not your job!'

'I know that! But I would love to prepare coffee for you, and I must tell you that I make very tasty coffee.' Tara insisted on preparing coffee for Kunal.

'Thanks, please go ahead!' Kunal said shrugging his shoulders. He had started changing his views about her.

After getting his cup of coffee, he again insisted that Tara should leave, but she made it clear that she was in no hurry to do so.

It was only when Kunal switched off his PC, locked the drawers and slipped his pen into its cover to call it a day that Tara too raised herself from her seat. She locked her fingers and stretched both arms upward saying, 'Yeah! I am feeling tired now.'

'I asked you to leave. Anyway, how will you go back alone at this time?' Kunal asked.

'I will hire an auto or a taxi, you will of course reimburse me the fare,' she said, without looking at Kunal. She seemed busy putting the mobile phone and the pen in her purse.

'I will do better, and drop you home myself, because it is not safe for you to travel alone at night,' said Kunal.

Tara could see her plan working well. Though she was quite used to travelling alone at night, she pretended to be quite naive before Kunal.

'Yes, you are right. The rising cases of crime against women are a blot on the face of our country's development. If women are not safe in Metros then what to talk of smaller places, where the law and order situation is yet more questionable! In fact, even I was thinking of asking for a lift from you. But...'Tara said with her eyes cast down.

'But what, Tara? Why couldn't you ask me for a lift?' asked Kunal.

'I felt a bit awkward asking for a favor,' said Tara.

'Am I a stranger before whom you cannot put your

genuine request?'he asked.

Tara said, 'Stranger…? Who said so? Rather, I wanted to tell you that you feel so familiar and look so handsome! I mean, I am sorry, I am being too forward.'

Kunal could not hold back his emotions at Tara's smooth talk and the flattery worked in Tara's favor. But he still pretended to be formal and said, 'Please feel free to ask for any kind of help!' Tara knew she had hit the mark.

Kunal drove to drop Tara home. Despite all his efforts to maintain a stiff upper lip, he was quite swept away by Tata's flattery. All the while he was driving he looked at his face, sometimes in the rear view mirror, sometimes in the side view mirrors of his car. His heart was in seventh heaven after hearing the words of compliment from a pretty and hot babe. The formal, official relation was changing to a passionate bond, and the two of them were seen with each other on most occasions.

Even sages gave up before the temptations of a woman, Kunal was only a human being. Her advances were well received by him. Slowly and gradually, the time they spent together increased. From attending meetings, to having lunch, and even having dinner together.

And one day, the inevitable happened. All the staff had left, and even Sitaram had gone after locking the office gate. Kunal and Tara were the last ones to move out of the building. They got into the lift, and the moment the lift started, Tara stumbled and fell on Kunal standing next to her. Kunal embraced her to prevent her fall. The two of them were so close that Tara's hot lips touched his bare skin as he did not button up his collar. She lifted her eyes to look into his, and their lips got entangled in a passionate kiss.

Since that day, Kunal was completely smitten by Tara. He became blind to all her mistakes, to an extent that he forgot his family. Tara was becoming his weakness, and he could not refuse her anything.

The launch of the new product became a launching pad for Tara in Kunal's life. She had emerged as a new favorite and also the winner of his favors. He had started enjoying her company as most of the time the two of them worked together. The successful launch of the product was followed by a promotion for Kunal and his package became double. On his recommendation, Tara was made a manager reporting to him directly.

Tara's entry into Kunal's life ruined his family life because Tara became his world, even more important than his child.

TWENTY-NINE

KUNAL INSERTED THE duplicate key to open the door, but the door slid open without resistance. Suman, in her frustrated mental state had forgotten to lock the door.

Kunal went mad. He made a big issue out of this instance to point out Suman's carelessness. He shouted at top of his voice, 'Suman how careless are you? You know about the crimes in the city and still you have not locked the door.'

Suman too burned with the fury of indignation. She replied, 'Why need you shout so much? Don't you know Kusum is sleeping?'

Kunal, with already a bone to pick with Suman, just flew off the handle, hearing Suman answer back so rudely.

'Suman, staying back at home has made you forget your culture and manners! How could you create a scene at the party by slapping Tara? You didn't slap her, rather you affronted me.'

'And Kunal, you are least bothered about my insult! The way you interacted with that lady made people believe that she was your wife and I was the caretaker.'

'Suman, mind your language.'

'Why should only I mind my language, why don't you mind your behavior?'

'Suman, Tara is just my colleague. If she looks hot and sexy then it is not her fault! If people find me pairing well with her then what do I do? And you? Your jealousy and inferiority complex made you stoop to a level that you created a scene before the world by slapping her! What was her fault?'

Kunal's words sounded like a hot iron rod scarring her soul. Even after her relentless service and affection, he had bypassed her for a female's physical attraction!

Kunal went on speaking, 'You don't try to impress me that what you are doing is something great! It was your own choice to stay back and manage your household, because to face the challenges of the world that is outside your home is not everyone's cup of tea. You are basically a lazy person and that is why you chose to stay back at home and enjoy the fruits of my hard work. You know how hard I have worked to reach this position, and mind you, it was

Tara who was beside me through this journey to attain this coveted position in my office. The things you do for me… cooking…cleaning, laundry etc...even a maid can be hired to do all this…!' Kunal was shouting without being bothered about the impact his words made on Suman. 'Oh my god!' he said, pulling his hair with his hands. 'What a lousy wife I have had to bear all my life!'

It was all a bit too much for Suman to bear. She felt her heart would burst. She shouted with all her might, 'How come you compared me to a maid in the house. It's that lady for whom you are stooping so low; I call her worse than a whore, a slut...!'

Kunal could abuse Suman, but he could not listen to any bad name being used for Tara. 'Suman…and there was a sudden, fast motion in the air, leading to a heavy sound and Kunal's hand rested on Suman's cheek giving her a hard blow. She fell on the floor, the last spark in her ending with tears. Her confidence was shattered; she wondered whether it could ever come to life again!

The ship was under threat of wreckage by the very people in whose service it was! It was the ship's crew who could have guided the ship out of the storm, but it was they who were putting it into turbulent waters. A curtain of darkness had engulfed the beacon which used to guide its way.

The minor clashes, disagreements, even heated

arguments between a husband and wife are a common, universal phenomenon. Such disagreements are said to add spice to the love life, but this case was different! It involved the entry of a third person in their life, whose entry could do nothing other than sabotage the entity of their beautiful family; the family that was her beautiful dream. The dream broke; it was soundless—but the void created and the fragments piercing her heart could allow her do nothing except clean the wound with her tears.

THIRTY

'MEMSAAB...MAIN JATI hoon, baby ne nashta kar liya hai mera kaam khatam ho gaya hai', the maid loudly informed Suman that she was leaving after finishing her work.

Suman lifted her head from the floor with some effort. Her head was feeling heavy and painful. She looked around for the maid. Sunlight sieved through the side of the curtains concealing the window, indicating it was already forenoon. She tried to raise her head further to have a look at the wall clock to know the exact time. Her head whirled with tremendous pain and her hand automatically reached for the painful spot on her forehead. The previous night's incident played like a recorded film before her eyes. She used her hand to clear her eyes, and could feel her forehead hurting too much.

The house carried traces of the previous night's happenings; pieces of the broken vase, which Kunal had thrown in his umbrage, and the pillows, bed sheet, mattress scattered all over the room, which Suman had thrown in retaliation.

Suman kept lying on the floor. To make things look normal, she started asking, 'Chinta, have you cleaned all the rooms?'

'Jee memsaab. I have cleaned everything, given breakfast to baby because she was crying. Your room still needs to be done, as I thought not to disturb you. Sirjee left without having anything!' The maid gave a detailed account. With some hesitation, she bent closer to Suman and asked in a low tone, 'Madamjee, is everything all right?'

Without even bothering for a response, she muttered, twisting her lips,'High class or low class, whatever be the status…men will be men, casual and careless. How would this world have existed without women, who sacrifice everything caring for the family?'

Chinta could understand everything without even needing to know from her mistress what went on in the house the previous night!

'Yeah! No, I mean everything is fine! Actually, I had backache, so I thought it was better to sleep on the floor, to get some relief!' Chinta looked at Suman and sniggered with a sarcastic smile. Suman didn't look at her, and gave her few more instructions for cleaning the room.

Suman headed for the washroom. She couldn't have prevented the maid from knowing about the previous night's fight; every article in the room narrated the story. Suman knew fully well that if she shared things verbally, it would be news to feed the rumor mills of the entire neighborhood.

The maid had put back the things in order. But how could she join the broken pieces of her heart, which hurt with greater intensity than at the time of the fight. Who could put her life back in order?

The memories ached like blisters on the heart and mind. Howsoever Suman tried she could not take her mind off from whatever happened the previous night! She was successful in avoiding the maid's questions but how could she avoid herself!

With her mind still besieged by the previous night's happenings, she rose up and went to look for Kusum who was playing with her toys in her room.

She dragged her steps towards the hall and sank on the cushioned sofa; she pulled the curtains over the windows, switched off the lights to avoid any brightness in the room, and closed her eyes, resting her head on the back of the sofa. The spark of love in Kunal's eyes, that had kindled her small world, was put out.

Her beautiful world was in eternal darkness. This darkness invaded her spirit and led her to an abysmal level of depression, she forgot about her own shadow, her little darling daughter.

With everything still intact, for her life had changed completely.

THIRTY-ONE

FOR SUMAN, LIFE ahead seemed like a journey devoid of charm; she could think of death as the only respite. Her life had reached a point where she could feel an unexplained vacuum that sucked all her energy. She was unable to decide what she should do! She was like a tired traveller who had no energy left for continuing the journey because the faith in the destination was lost.

Suman opened her eyes when she heard Kusum crying. After searching for Suman in all the rooms she came to the hall and there she found her mother reclining on the sofa. When she did not get any response to her wailing and shouting, she pulled Suman with all the force she had.

'Mamma, Mamma, listen Mamma!' Kusum was shaking Suman while screaming and crying.

Suman got perturbed at Kusum pulling her so abruptly and her irritation reached its peak; she slapped Kusum and shook her hard.'Why can't you let me be in peace for some time. You have had your breakfast, what more do you want? Can't you play on your own for some time.'

Kusum started sobbing.With tears flowing rapidly, she said, 'Sorry ma..ma. I was frightened to see a cockroach in my room. I am feeling quite hungry also. You have not made me eat my lunch.'

Suman regained her consciousness. "Oh my god!" she said to herself.

She looked up at the clock; it was already evening.

She was not able to reason out what was happening to her. She tried to get back to her senses; she was punishing her child because she wanted to punish Kunal. She cursed herself for her misbehavior, and pulled Kusum towards her to cuddle her and kissed her on the cheek where she had hit her. Suman too cried with Kusum.

Suman was filled with remorse for ill-treating her child. She said, 'Kusum, today I will do whatever you ask me to do.' She kissed her on her forehead. Kusum had stopped crying but still whimpered in a low tone. 'What do you want, Kusum?' asked Suman.

Kusum said, 'Nothing! I don't want anything.'

'Your Mamma is bad!' Suman said looking penitent.

'I know you are still angry with me.' Suman held both her ears with her hands and said, 'Sorry baby. I am really very, very sorry.' Tears still flowed from Suman's eyes.

The little child couldn't see her mother upset; she wiped the tears from her mother's face and hugged her saying, 'Mamma I want to go to the park!'

'Ok darling! Let's first eat something then we will surely go to the park.'

Suman hurriedly prepared some cheese sandwiches and gave them to Kusum. Kusum lifted one sandwich from her plate and brought it near Suman saying, 'Mamma you have not had anything since morning, please have this.' She brought the sandwich near Suman's mouth with her small chubby hands.

Suman was inundated once again by waves of emotion and said 'I'm not hungry darling! You please finish it fast or it will get dark and we will not be able to go to the park.'

Kusum was also determined to feed her mother before she ate anything so she said 'no,' by turning her face away from her mother. 'I won't eat anything until you too eat some sandwiches.' Suman had to yield to her request.

Suman was overwhelmed by her daughter's concern. There was one more soul on this earth, besides her parents, who had concern for her. How innocent are these children, uncorrupted by the evilness of this world! Their hearts so pure and gentle that all those who come in their contact are purified. After feeding Kusum, Suman tied her hair, locked the house and went to the park.

The evening was the time when children gathered in the park accompanied by a grown up; their parents, grandparents, or their caretakers like servants or drivers. The kids became busy playing games or doing activities of their choice; some rode bicycles, some enjoyed swings, or played games of their choice. The dearth of open space in houses, if not fully, at least partially made mothers bring children to the park.

Suman stretched her legs, folded her arms and rested her head on the back support of the grilled iron bench to look towards the sky. At times, she tried to divert her attention by concentrating on the beautiful park and Kusum. The park had patches carved in geometrical shapes made colorful with dahlias, marigolds, and most of the varieties of verbenas. The grilled iron benches were fixed in between the flower patches. The colorful hues in the garden, though, could not have made her colorless life beautiful, but they did try to lighten up the black patches of her life briefly. She touched the flowers to feel their gentleness and freshness. Then she lifted her eyes to look for Kusum. Seeing her daughter dance and prance from one swing to another made Suman feel a little better. Her gaze followed her for some time; thereafter her deep seated unhappy thoughts again hijacked her senses.

She was again with Kunal. She had merged herself so much with him that not a moment passed without his thought in her mind. The memories of the good and happy time they had spent together captured her mind.

What is this noise all about? Suddenly an uproar of sounds deflected her attention.

She saw a small crowd in one corner of the park. The security guard with a long baton and mouthful of rebukes was chasing some boys. And then her eyes fell on a good number of crushed flowers and a few uprooted plants on the grass around one patch of flowers. And Suman could put two and two together; the flowers must have been brutally plucked from the tender plants, and after plucking, the ill-mannered boys even crushed some of the flowers.

After chasing the hooligans out of the park, Anaram, the watchman on the society's payroll was back in his chair. Suman got up from the bench and came to Anaram to find out what had happened.

He started narrating the entire episode! 'A few girls were strolling in the garden, and a group of boys followed them. The boys ruthlessly plucked flowers from the plants, and threw them on the girls. While plucking they even uprooted some plants. They badly trampled the entire patch. I don't know what would they would haved one had I been late even by five more minutes.' Anaram was furious.

Anaram said, 'Bibijee, I had just gone away from here for a few minutes to attend to nature's call and those guys, the ruffians, got an opportunity to get inside the park. Look how they have spoilt the park within no time. How hard Devu the gardener has worked to make this park look beautiful. I have never seen such a passion for one's job in anybody; he has reaped all the saplings like his children to make this park beautiful for everyone. How upset he will be to see one patch ruined!'

While Anaram spoke, Suman's mind was on Kusum. She was making a comparison between the flowers and Kusum. Anaram's words were becoming obscured in the anxiety developing in her mind for her child.

She looked around in all directions to see where her daughter was. She could not wait for him to finish his sentence and moved on abruptly saying a few soothing words to him.

'Fine Anaram! Be more watchful from now on, and put someone else on alert even if you have to move out for a few minutes. Certainly, Devu will be upset! Even I am upset, but what to do now? I can't see Kusum around; let me find out where she is.'

'Bibijee, shall I come with you to look for baby?'

'No...no,' Suman said. 'She must be here only! I shall find her.'

Anaram was a mobile walkie-talkie, very much like our current day media (which can make or mar the image of a person), with his extraordinary power of expression in his native vernacular language. He was also the storehouse of information of all houses in the building; he was known as the most active link of the grapevine. Given a chance to be heard he could have started with his endless stories about each house in the building. Before he could begin his latest gossip, Suman had already made a rush to look for her daughter. She started walking at a rapid pace towards the swings.

Where was Kusum?

Suman started thinking, "Isn't my pretty daughter like these pretty flowers; if unattended, she is as vulnerable as these beautiful flowers." The more she thought, the more anxious she became for her daughter. She looked on both sides to see where Kusum was.

'Mamma,' Kusum's voice called out from behind her.

"There she is," Suman sighed.

Kusum had a big smile on her face. She was holding the hand of a girl, who was almost of her age. She chuckled, 'Mamma, this is my friend Pari.'

Before Suman could ask a question about Pari, Kusum gave complete information about her friend. 'She is my class friend. She studies in my school. She stays in Sitara building.'Suman too had to smile! Her guilt subsided looking at her happy daughter.

'Ok! That means Pari studies in your school and she stays nearby,' Suman said.

'Mamma, she comes to the park daily, and you never bring me here. Now I will come to the park every day!' Kusum had a genuine complaint and a demand.

Suman used to be busy in shopping, then cooking in the evenings. Though the park was within visible distance from her house, she never allowed Kusum to go there alone.

'Ok, done!' Suman said.

'Let me at least know something more from Pari.' Suman came down on her knees, on the tuft of green grass, to bring herself down to Pari's level. She asked her, 'Have you come to the park alone?'

'No, aunty, I have come with my Mom.' Before Suman could ask any more questions, a beautiful hand was before her extended for a handshake.

'Hi! I am Pari's Mom, Arunima.' The lady's voice fell on Suman's ear.

Suman turned to look at the face of the lady. She sounded quite familiar. Suman was dumbstruck momentarily. She rotated her body to face Arunima and almost shouted, 'Anu, it's you, here, how come?'

Arunima took a step forward and embraced her, 'Suman

even I can't believe it! Oh my god! We are meeting after such a long time.'

'Anu you have not changed a wee bit,' Suman said. Arunima was wearing jeans and a casual blue T-shirt! Only the length of her hair had grown till her shoulders, which she had tied up in a ponytail. She had applied a shade of light pink lipstick and looked calm and serene.

'Anu, your looks have not changed but your personality has changed completely. Where is that chirpy Anu?'

Anu, looking down at the ground below said with a quiet smile, 'Darling, I am a mother now. I need to be a little serious.'

The kids were delighted to see that their mothers were friends just as they were! 'Can we go and play?' They both asked their mothers together in a chorus.

Both Suman and Arunima nodded to them. They smiled, held hands, and moved on with galloping steps towards the swings.

Suman and Arunima positioned themselves on a nearby iron bench to continue chatting, while their eyes supervised their daughters' playing.

Suman asked Arunima, 'Anu I think we spoke just once after we left the institute. I think you shifted your residence, and even your mobile number had an "out of service" message. We both became busy in our lives and lost touch completely. It has been such a long time, and I have so much to share with you; I'm sure even you have lots to share with me. Remember, how we knew every detail of each other's life at the Institute.'

'Yeah Suman, I have much to speak about, but mine is a long story and I shall share with you every minor detail, but the condition is that you will have to come to my house.' Anu looked happier than she was a few moments ago.

Suman had to accept the offer.

'But I can't promise you about the day,' Suman said.

'Ok, sweetheart!' Anu looked a little amused.

'And what about you Suman? What has been your story of these past years?' Anu asked.

Suman did not want to upset Anu with the story of her domestic problems so she nodded and said, 'Yeah, I have become a full-time mom and a home manager. I will tell you when we sit together.'

Both turned their attention back to their daughters. Suman felt quite light hearted after spending some time with Arunima. Though their discussion centered on their daughters, but Suman felt that she had let off steam that had built up within her. May be for some moments only but her mind was away from Kunal and the other lady in Kunal's life. Meeting Anu blew away much of her blues.

Suman and Kusum were walking back from the park

as usual holding hands when suddenly Kusum looked towards Suman and asked, 'Mamma, I want to unlock our gate today.'

'Why Kusum?'

'Mamma please, let me do it! Please, just for today. I just feel like doing it. I am not a kid, please Mamma!'

Suman looked at her daughter, saying with a smile, 'Okay, I know you are not a kid when you are out of the home. But the moment you are back at home you become a small baby who needs mamma beside her for every little thing!'

Kusum puckered up her nose and folded her hands saying, 'Please, Mamma. I will not act as a kid while at home also, Mamma...promise.'

'Ok,' said Suman.

She took the keys out of her purse and gave them to Kusum, who rushed towards the door to open it.

Kusum kept her hand on the door but it opened on a slight thrust. And Suman could see that Kusum had rushed inside shouting something.

She followed her with hurried steps, not being able to make out what had happened.

As she entered her house, she was taken aback to see Kunal sitting on the sofa with the newspaper open in front of him. By the time Suman reached inside, Kusum was in

Kunal's lap. She was so excited to be in her father's lap, kissing him incessantly. Suman looked at her daughter and knew why children are called angels!

Kunal looked towards Suman to make eye contact. Maybe he was in a mood to make truce with her!

Why was her husband behaving like a changed man? But she, unlike her daughter, could not forget anything! The mental torture, the insult, she might not forget till her dying day. She turned away and moved towards the kitchen.

Suman served the food in three plates on the table, without bothering to know whether Kunal wanted to have dinner or not.

He was looking at Suman, but Suman avoided eye contact with him. So he chose his daughter as a medium to communicate with his wife. 'Kusum, you know Papa is going to Singapore tomorrow. What shall I get for you from Singapore.'

Kusum made an innocent face and told him, 'Papa, why don't you take me and Mamma along with you? I also want to go to Singapore!'

Kunal picked up Kusum in his lap and said, 'It's my promise, I will take you both with me next time. Ok!'

Kusum placed her hand in her dad's, and said,'Ok.'

'But my darling you will have to do me a favor. Please ask your Mom to pack my bag the way she has been doing earlier. I will stay there for 5-7 days depending on the circumstances,' Kunal said looking at Kusum,

Kusum kept nodding at her father, and looked towards Suman, as if pleading on her father's behalf.

Suman, without looking towards Kunal, made a gesture of approval to Kusum. Kusum jumped from Kunal's lap and rushed towards Suman, pulled her down holding her hand, and gave her a peck on the cheek.

Kunal wanted to cheer up Suman, but it would not be easy! He knew that she was deeply hurt due to his unpardonable act. All the while, he kept looking at her face as if begging for a smile. But Suman's ever smiling face looked stoic and sad. This destroyed the charm of their beautiful home. Kunal wished to have his flight postponed, but alas, things don't always move as per one's wishes.

The flight was scheduled for the very next day. Since he had to move to office with his baggage to travel directly to the airport from office, he had to leave for office at his usual time. He knew, that a one-word apology, wouldn't work because his was not just a simple mistake.

Before leaving, he picked Kusum up in his lap to bid her goodbye; and he utilized this opportunity to make truce with his wife. He said, 'Suman, take care.'

Suman replied coldly for the sake of her daughter, 'Ok.'

THIRTY-TWO

THOUGH KUNAL HAD hardly been meeting his daughter for the last few days but the news of Kunal being away to Singapore made Kusum quite sad. Suman could not bear Kusum's sadness.

Kunal being away, Suman thought she had lots of free time as she did not have to bother much about household chores.

She instantly thought of a plan. She thought she would go to Anu's house. "We will be together after such a long time, sharing our life's stories. I also need to know what made Anu change so much. She looks so different from her original self. Yeah, I can also plan an outing with Anu and Pari joining us, and I'm sure this will make Kusum very happy."

She decided to go to Arunima's house before Kusum was back from school.

Then she remembered the new coffee shop near Kusum's bus stop and became happier thinking, "Anu and I can have coffee and spend time chatting at the coffee shop; in this way, we can also pick up Kusum and Pari when they are back."

After meeting Arunima, the growing despondency and pessimism within her petered out like the darkness gradually reduces on the burning of a candle. Suman was walking towards Arunima's apartment thinking that it was solely her own fault; why had she let her happiness become caged in the enclosure of Kunal's expectations? Like the clever priests and the clergymen have imprisoned God and spiritualism in the realms of religious fundamentalism and rigid rituals; media pundits, brand managers and businessmen with pecuniary interest have trapped beauty in various definitions and criteria. She had tried to meet every expectation of Kunal to make her home an abode of happiness, at the cost of her own well-being.

Her heart was now free of all the self-imposed restrictions that if she displeased her husband, her family life would be ruined! What if she crushes her personality? Will she be able to take care of her family better?

She tried to shove aside the spiralling waves of thoughts within her head. By that time, she reached Anu's apartment.

"Thank god, I have reached Arunima's house." She checked the house number—401. "Yes, this is what Arunima had told me. I should have checked the house number before leaving. What a fool I am! In my excitement of meeting a long lost friend I even forgot to update her phone number." Suman's lips twisted into a smile. She was thanking her destiny that had brought her so close to her friend at a point when she needed her.

"Well, I hope this is Anu's house. I remember pretty well that she mentioned this number. I can trust my memory. I am not that old that I forget things," she thought and smiled. She waited outside Arunima's house after ringing the doorbell. But there was no sound of any movement happening in response to the bell. She checked whether the door was locked. No, there was no lock on the door. She rang the bell again, and looked at her wristwatch to check the time.

It was 10 am. "Arunima might be taking her bath, or maybe...." Instead of making any guesses she preferred waiting. She was already tired of the waves of thoughts and didn't want to involve herself in any more thinking. She just wanted to see Anu's reaction at her surprise visit to her home.

She was busy remembering the days she was with Anu at the Institute, when she heard the footsteps walking towards the door.

The doorknob squeaked, and the door opened with a creaking sound.

Suman's mouth had opened to say so many things, but once opened it remained in that state without a single word coming from her. The expression on her face changed like a litmus paper in reaction to the acid solution. Her eyes filled with tears and she turned around and started running towards the lift.

THIRTY-THREE

KUNAL SAT ON a chair in the lounge after reporting at the airline counter. He was waiting for his colleagues to arrive. It was a three-member team consisting of Tara, Aditya and himself, who were going for the South Asia trip to finalize a mega deal.

He looked at his watch, only an hour more was left for reporting. Since there was hardly anything else to do, at that moment, Kunal tried to fix his gaze at the café in front of him. There was a newly-wed couple. The young man sat quite close to his pretty wife. They were sipping their ice-cream shake with two straws from the same glass. The man had put one hand around his wife's back while his other hand cupped her hands holding the ice cream glass. Her hands carried the imprint of henna. She also wore '*chuda*' (the bangles used in Punjabi weddings). A beautiful diamond ring adorned her ring finger. Their faces were turned towards each other, lost in each other's eyes; they were oblivious of the activity at the airport. They probably were on their honeymoon trip.

Kunal's mind went to the sweet memories of his own marriage, and his gorgeous wife Suman, at the time of their marriage. The couple reminded him of the happy times he had spent with his wife.

Kunal, gifted with a handsome personality—tall, fair, and handsome, easily won the favors of females in his college. The girls were ready to die for him. He had befriended some of the girls in his college, but none of them he considered worthy of marriage. His dream girl had to be someone with lots of love in her heart.

It was the charm in Suman which had swept him off his feet. In their very first meeting his heart had decided to make her the queen of his life. Saloni's marriage offered a platform, where he and Suman could study each other's traits. The brief spark ignited with the skin deep beauty did not take long to change into a profound relationship. It was same for both of them; their intellect, character and every trait was acceptable to them. For Kunal, Suman was the only girl who fitted the bill; for him and for his mother too.

After the death of his father, he was the only support left for his mother, and he understood his responsibilities well. His dream girl had also to fit in the framework of his mother.

All the girls who studied with him had great plans for their career; family for them was not an immediate option. Those who seemed prepared to settle down for a family life were too pragmatic when it came to relationships.

Kunal wanted a wife who had the right blend of moral values, intellect and beauty. It was something of a similar story for Suman and her parents. Kunal's temperament, his family and his manners made him an excellent choice of Suman's parents for their daughter. His caring, witty and jovial nature endeared him to all who came in contact with him.

It was as a match made in heaven, and both partners seemed to cherish the blessings of God. Suman had made his life beautiful. He had a home like heaven, manned by his intelligent and beautiful wife. She had chosen to beautify her home with her love and intellect for his sake, and for the sake of their darling daughter.

"But what had he done to such a beautiful relationship, and for whom—Tara?" Kunal thought.

Aditya arrived to break the link of his thoughts. The two of them lined up in the queue before the boarding gate.

There was a heavy rush of passengers to board the flight.

Aditya said, 'We needed a little more preparation for the project.'

'You are correct, Adi, but who knew that there would be this political emergency, and if we do not have this deal finalized now, it will be a case of never. After elections, the new party will have other important issues on its agenda and our plans of making our product international might get stalled.'

Then suddenly, he seemed to remember something and groped in his coat pocket.

'What happened?' asked Aditya.

'Tara has not arrived! I'm looking for my mobile to call her up and find out where she is,' Kunal said looking a bit worried. 'She should have told me that she was not interested in this trip at the time we were getting the bookings done. With great difficulty I could manage three seats. You know how popular Singapore is as a tourist destination!'

'Did she tell you she was not willing to come?' asked Aditya.

'Not really; In fact, I have not even met her since the party day.'

'Then, how could she know about the changed schedule?'

'Well, I texted her the schedule, and sent her the printed copy of the ticket and the itenerary through the office peon.' Kunal said this avoiding Aditya's eyes because he was telling a lie. He was feeling embarrassed to share with Aditya that he had gone mad for a lady to the extent of spoiling his own family life.

THIRTY-FOUR

THE SCENE OF the fight with Suman hovered in his mind.

Tara did not come to office the next day, after the party. Kunal tried to reach her through the office phone and with his mobile.He had been calling persistently, but she was not reachable.

"Maybe she is still upset about her insult at the party! But I apologized to her so many times." Then, he got a message from the reception that Tara's son was not well, so she was not able to come to office. "If she could not show up, she could at least have spoken to me," Kunal thought.

Then he checked the fax, and there was an urgent fax marked to him that their visit was preponed and they had to leave by next evening's flight. 'Heavens!' said Kunal, holding his head between his two hands. He didn't know how to handle this.

The product, which was Kunal's brainchild had performed extraordinarily well in the Indian market. Now the company was targeting the South East Asian market. Though there were many international contenders, but no other Indian company was in the running.

Since the product was all Kunal's, he was also given charge of handling of its international affairs. But, to introduce it in the international market and to team up with the global market leaders, minor modifications were required to be made, which only Kunal was aware of. The changes were required—both on the cost and the quality front. Kunal had put in his heart and soul in doing research for the product, and had made a report by highlighting the nuances of his product that were to be for the advantage of the foreign market. The details were worked out with such finesse that the deal had to come to them.

He was allowed to select his team to assist him on this. Tara was his obvious choice. All the information was kept strictly confidential to the core team, i.e Aditya and Tara. Tara's absence created a crisis for Kunal.

But, before this Tara had not taken any leave, not even for a day! Kunal kept guessing the reasons for her absence. "May be her son is seriously ill," Kunal thought. "But why would she keep her mobile off? Maybe she is still upset at Suman for her behavior at the party!" And this thought made him go wild at Suman again. He thought that only Suman was at fault! He was convinced that Tara did not deserve that treatment, and Suman should have behaved properly with her. But, as much as he knew Tara, he was sure that she was a very practical lady, and she would overlook such issues for the sake of her work.

The HR team managed to prepone the tickets, and sent the tickets to Kunal. He opened them to check the exact departure time. He called up Aditya and asked him to pick up his ticket from him.

"How about Tara? Let me go personally to her house to hand over the tickets, and know exactly what is holding her back at home," Kunal thought. He could have sent the tickets through the peon too, but then his emotional bonding with her made him decide to go personally. He left office quite early and thought of completing minor nitty gritties the next morning. Since Tara would also be with him it would be a lot easier to give final touches to the work before leaving. He would come to office early next morning and move to the airport straight from there.

He had dropped Tara home, many a times, but he never went inside her house. He reached her house and made a quick entry through the small porch to ring the bell, but the sight he saw through the glass window shook him. The door was not bolted and remained open with a slit. He waited outside for a while, trying to understand what was going on inside the house.

A man was sitting on the sofa with his back facing the entrance. He had kept his legs crossed on the glass table in the center of the room. He was smoking a cigarette and blowing smoke puffs with his head resting on the sofa back. A lady, about 23-25 years old was holding both the hands of a child reprimanding him in harsh words. When she lifted her hand to slap the child, Kunal could not restrain himself and forced the door open.

Seeing Kunal, the lady's grip loosened, and the child started crying loudly. Kunal went near the child and picked him up.

'Who are you?' The lady asked in a stern voice.The man on the sofa had also risen up to support the lady.

Instead of replying to them, Kunal asked, 'Where is your Madam?'

'Madam!' asked the maid. 'Madam must be in the office, but who are you to inquire like this?'

'Shut up! You…' Kunal's anger had gone through the roof. 'Whoever I am, how dare you touch the child? Let me just report to the police!'

The lady got intimidated thinking Kunal to be someone

close to or known to Tara. 'No no sir! Sorry sir! I mean, I was trying to make him have his food. Sir, he has not had anything since morning, and Madam has asked me to feed him anyway I can. Madam has to go somewhere for a week tomorrow, and she has to finish the preparations by today evening.'

'Is this the way to feed the child? And he will be alone with you for the entire week!'

Kunal was confused. He started thinking what kind of woman Tara was? Didn't she know how her maid treated the child? And then, where had she gone? By taking leave on the pretext of her son's illness, where was she the entire day? And how did Tara come to know that they were leaving the next day for a week? How had she come to know about the preponement of our trip, when she did not come to office? Did she call up Aditya? But Aditya would have updated him about any such conversation with Tara, and no one other than Aditya and he knew about the advanced date. Maybe, in that case, someone from HR must have informed her.

Kunal kept quiet for a few moments and the maid replied to his question. 'No sir, his Dad will be coming tomorrow to pick him up.'

'Pick him up! Meaning? Where does his Dad live?'

'I don't know where he lives? But Madam and Sir don't live together. They are divorced.'

Kunal was taken aback for a while, as Tara had never told him about the divorce.

The child was still crying bitterly. His little fingers pressed against Kunal's shoulders and the tears kept flowing. He patted the child's back and tried to soothe him with sweet words, 'I will get you some chocolates of your choice. Tell me which chocolate do you like?'

The child was not ready to leave Kunal and he clung to him tightly as he felt secure in his arms. 'To feed him, do you need to hit him?' asked Kunal. 'Why don't you admit that he was being a disturbance for you both?' Turning towards the ruffian like man he asked.

But the man had already left by that time.

'Sir, he is my fiancé! Sometimes he comes to meet me.'

'And you have taken permission from your Madam for him to visit you during her absence. Isn't it? What are you being paid for? To attend to your guests or look after the child! Just remember, if ever I find this happening again you will be with the police and of course you know what will happen after that.'

'I will not do it again, sir. But sir, may I know who you are…? I mean, what will I tell Madam about you?'

Kunal handed over the tickets to the lady and said, 'Give this to your Madam, and she will know! And also ask her to call me to confirm that she has received the tickets. And why is her mobile not working? Do you have any other number on which I can contact her?'

'No idea, Sir. I don't have her mobile number. She only calls up to talk to the baby.'

Kunal waited for some time. The child was calm. Kunal asked him, 'Do you want chocolates?' He remembered that Suman always kept some chocolates for Kusum in the car. How she cared for the smallest of their needs, both Kusum's and his!

'Yes,' the child said.

He asked him to wait and went towards the car to get the chocolates. But as he was near the door again, he could hear the maid softly telling the child, 'Do not tell anything to this man, or your father, otherwise Bhiku will burn your fingers with cigarette stubs. Ok! so don't utter a word.'

Kunal felt quite helpless! If he tried to help the child, his condition would become yet more miserable. And then he wondered why the maid did not warn the child against not sharing things with his mother. May be Tara was aware of everything happening to the child in her absence; or, maybe, she was hardly bothered how her child was being treated. But whatever was the case, he could not have helped the child much. He entered the room pretending that he was just not aware of anything happening in the closed room.

'Sir, please come and have tea. I was asking baba whether

he will have his food or not. I have to finish his packing by evening as tomorrow morning his father will come to pick him up,' the maid said humbly.

A short visit to Tara's house had revealed countless skeletons in her cupboard. He was unable to decide what kind of person Tara was! How could she trust an illiterate, slow-witted person to handle her most prized possession—her child? May be after the presentation he would talk to Tara to tell her what was happening behind her back. He thought of advising her to look after her child properly.

And while driving back to his house, he kept thinking of Kusum and Suman. This time he saw his wife in a different light. The glass of Tara's enchantement had broken and he could perceive things and events more clearly.

THIRTY-FIVE

SUMAN WALKED BRISKLY towards the lift followed by a male voice, 'Please Suman, stop. Just stop for a moment; listen to me.'

But Suman did not stop until she was halted by a strong hand that held her by her wrist and pulled her back.

She turned to look at the person holding her hand and asked, 'What do you want from me, Rajan? You have punished me enough.'

'Suman,' Rajan said, 'Will you not give me one chance to explain my case?'

'What case, Rajan?' Something wrenched at Suman's heart and she pushed his hand aside to move away from him.

'Suman please! I beg you to listen to me just for few minutes, for the sake of the feelings we had for each other, and then decide my case.'

Suman was forced to look at Rajan's face. His eyes looked pure and profound as earlier. His face still looked calm and attractive, but with a stubble.

She could not control her tears and said looking into his eyes, 'Listen to whom Rajan and for what? I don't want to listen to any of your stories. And, by the way, what feelings are you talking about? You never had any feelings for me! You and Anu being in a relationship is beyond my wildest imagination. I would never have let you be in my life knowing that you loved Anu. Had you told me that you liked someone else, I wouldn't have undergone the mental torture! Why did you play games with me?'

'Suman, will you stop imagining things. Will you give me just one chance to explain?If you have decided to term me a culprit, then I will continue to live in the guilt I have been living in till now! And let me tell you that destiny played the game in which I have been the loser.' Rajan's voice had become heavy and full of pain.

Suman fixed her eyes on Rajan's face to judge whether he was telling the truth or not! Rajan still had the same honesty on his face as he had when she met him for the first time.

He said, 'I owe you an explanation. Please listen to me and then you can charge me with any allegation you wish.'

Suman agreed to listen to Rajan who suggested that

they go to the same café near the bus stop, where Suman had planned to go with Anu. That way they could pick up their daughters from the bus stop.

'Who is Pari? Is she Avinash's child, or Rajan's? She should be Rajan's child, otherwise why would Rajan nurture someone else's child? Then, what had happened to Avinash's child?' Layers were being uncovered from Suman's own past, and she didn't know what should be her reaction to them!

Suman inquired, 'Rajan, where is Arunima? I mean, she is your wife now!'

'She left this morning for her week long residential meditation session. She attends these sessions every year, and I have to take leave during that period to look after Pari. And your other questions can be answered only if you listen to me—my story that I wish to tell you!'

'What happened to Arunima?' asked Suman. 'Is she suffering from some problem?'

Rajan looked at Suman and said, 'Shall we go to the cafe?'

Suman and Rajan sat quietly after placing the order for the coffee, and then Rajan started.

'Suman, I don't know from where to start the complex story of my life! Ok, let me start from our International project. Do you remember that international project, and our whole team slogging day in and day out for its successful completion?'

'Yes! How can I forget that?' said Suman. 'But, what is its relevance now?'

'Suman, why have you started taking whatever I say with a pinch of salt? Of course there must be some reason why I mention that project?'

Suman felt embarrassed at her rudeness and said, 'Sorry, Rajan, Please tell me!'

'That project was the T junction of my life where I was forced to turn into the direction opposite to where I wanted to go.'

Rajan went into the flashback of his days when he and Suman worked at Maryland Inc.

'I had prepared a draft of the project report with its estimated completion date, and with it, I went to the MD's room to announce that it would, at the most, take a month to begin the production under international collaboration. We were in the middle of the discussion when there was an urgent call on the MD's hotline number. While talking on the phone, deep lines of worry started appearing on the MD's forehead. After finishing his talk, he became quiet and deeply absorbed in thought as if he was in dire straits.'

I was unable to control my anxiety and asked, 'Sir, if you don't mind, may I ask you about the phone call which has left you so worried.'

Our MD then shared, 'Thanks Rajan, I will certainly

share my problem, and I also feel confident that you will be in a position to help me out with some solution to the crisis.'

I had said, 'Sir, your problem is our problem and whatever possible I can do to help I shall do!'

He then shared that there was an emergency in Gujarat because of the disturbance in the law and order situation of the state. This had caused a serious threat to our production unit located in Vadodra. The person heading the plant, which was the company's main profit center, belonged to a minority community. There was also a serious threat to the life of our plant in-charge, Mr Mukhtar.

In fact, Mr Mukhtar had caught four men bungling the company's funds. He had dismissed them for their misconduct and they had found a way to take revenge on him.

'The breakout of communal riots in Gujarat had given them a good chance of settling their scores with Mr Mukhtar. He had received a letter of threat to kill him and his family, and also that the plant would be set on fire if at all he visited it or was seen near the plant. The mischief mongers were fomenting communal feeling in the factory employees to serve their own interest. There was an immediate need to save the factory and the life of Mr Mukhtar and his family. He requested me to do a favor for the company and him personally. And I could not say No.

'He asked me to leave for Gujarat immediately without letting anyone know about the plan. He feared that any such news could cause disturbance in other offices, and it could impact all our international projects in the pipeline.

'Without talking to anyone about our secret operation, I went to Gujarat which was reeling under the heat of communal violence. I reached the factory with the help of the special security force which could be arranged due to our MD's high level contacts. My presence placated the employees, who too were under the influence of the mob. The communal feeling had overpowered the minds of the majority of the population and at that point of time they had even forgotten their brotherly terms with their neighbors.'

'The employees were brainwashed against Mr Mukhtar and they looked at all his actions and decisions through the communal glass. Understanding the delicacy of the situation, I moved to the company rest house and went to visit him secretly at dusk. Mr Mukhtar had no children, and he lived with his wife at the bunglow within the company's precincts. Arunima, along with her mother was with Mr Mukhtar, her uncle, those days. Probably, her mother brought her there for her delivery. It was difficult for Arunima's mother to handle the delivery issue of her unwed daughter. Even though Arunima belongs to a family with a modern outlook, but still being part of a conservative society, they had to deal with the stigma attached to the legitimacy of the child's birth. Mr Mukhtar was a gentle soul, so was his wife, who was from Saudi Arabia. Arunima's mother trusted only her younger brother for support during her difficult times, and Mr Mukhtar and his wife welcomed her at their home, making the best arrangements for Arunima's delivery.' Rajan paused. He felt overwhelmed with grief.

Suman kept listening to Rajan without any questions and when he paused she asked him to continue, saying,

'Then? Then what happened?' Her curiosity grew with every sentence that Rajan spoke.

Rajan said, 'When I reached their house, the family seemed to be in tension, which was quite natural. I had gone to check the family's well-being and carried some cash for them as per the directions of our MD. But,I became concerned when I saw how fear and insecurity had gripped the family because Mr Mukhtar had received a warning letter to vacate the company bunglow, or else the miscreants mentioned they would set ablaze the factory complex.

'So, I decided to shift Mr Mukhtar's family along with Arunima and her mother to the company guest house, till an arrangement could be made to shift them to a safer place. I, along with Mr Mukhtar thought that it would be safe to shift only under the cover of darkness, so that no one could trace the whereabouts of the family. The servants were given leave and Mr Mukhtar and I decided to drive his two cars with their belongings to the guest house, which was on the outskirts of the city. It had less communal tension and a higher concentration of minority population. Mr Muktar and his wife were in one car, and he rode ahead of me because he was aware of the way. I followed him with Arunima and her mom in my car.

'We had hardly moved a kilometer when we saw a few men standing in the way of Mr Mukhtar's car. Probably some servant came to know of the plan and shared it with the miscreants. My car was still some distance away; two men with covered faces shot point blank at Mr Mukhtar and his wife.

Arunima and her mother panicked, and I put my car in the back gear and rushed back at top speed, taking the turn at the first available cut from the main road. Seeing her uncle and aunt being shot caused trauma to Arunima, and her labour pain started.

'It was such a terrible moment. But, thankfully, I could see a signboard of a hospital and took my car there. While I was arranging the stretcher by talking at the reception, Arunima's mom was with her consoling her daughter with words of strength, trying to put on a brave face. And Arunima was carried inside the hospital. I went near the car to bring her mother along, and also hand over the keys to the security guard for valet parking. I saw Arunima's mom sweating profusely and gasping for breath. Immediately, I called for another stretcher and she too was taken inside.

'Arunima was taken inside the operation theater and Arunima's mother had to be put in the ICU because she had suffered a massive heart attack. The doctors could control the situation for some time but they had no hopes of her recovering. Arunima's mom wanted to see me, and I was allowed to be in the ICU for some time. She called me closer to her, and took a promise from me that I would look after Arunima after her death. She pleaded with me with folded hands to look after Anu and her child till the time Anu could get over the recent shock. She uttered with great difficulty the story of Arunima and how she was ditched.

'I had to make a promise to fulfill her last wish for the sake of humanity, and the moment she had my words of assurance she breathed her last. Anu gave birth to Pari, and after few days I took her to the guest house along with me. Knowing about her mom's death and the scene of her uncle and aunt getting shot in front of her eyes put Anu under a terrible shock. She was panic-stricken and got psychotic at times. She started being afraid of even shadows and noise. It was difficult for me to control her and the baby. I had to be with her all the time and did not know what to do!

'I wanted to conceal the news of Anu being with me,

because human beasts were lurking all around looking for an opportunity to pounce upon any innocent being on the pretext of religion. But in small towns, it hardly takes time for news to spread like forest fire. The miscreants got to know that Arunima and Pari were with me. I was waiting for an opportunity to take them out of Gujarat but Anu's condition didn't let me do so.

'And the worst was still to come. At night when I heard noise all around the guesthouse. I peeped through the window to check what was happening outside and the scene made my blood run cold. A horde of people, armed with daggers, javelins and batons, were inching towards the guest house. I didn't know what to do then! May be, God, also could not bear to see so much injustice being done to one person, and an idea flashed in my mind.

'There was only one way in which I could save Arunima's life and that was by making her my wife and Pari my daughter. Only an association with me could have saved their lives. I went out alone to face the crowd. The security guards were not able to control them. I had asked the group what they wanted. They said that they would not let any person from the minority community stay there, not even a child. My heart wailed to see the extent of darkness that had clouded the souls and minds of the perpetrators who had forgotten how they would face God on the Day of Judgment.

I boldly confronted the crowd and said that there was no one from the other community staying in the guest house.'

'Then what about the lady and the child?' a bald, robust looking man leading the crowd asked?

'The lady is my wife and it is our child,' I said.

'The unruly crowd was not ready to buy my argument. They demanded that they take a look at the lady to decide whether I spoke the truth or not! I requested the crowd to wait. Again my mind was in confusion—what if they had seen Arunima before at Mr Mukhtar's place? I left everything to god and went inside to bring Arunima out before the crowd. I held her hand and as I passed the lounge area my eyes fell on the rangoli decorated before Lord Ganesha's statue. And something clicked; if Arunima had red color in her hair parting, the crowd would be assured that she was a Hindu married lady. I lifted a pinch of the red powder and immediately covered the parting in Arunima's hair with it.

I took her out before the crowd and as I had guessed, the crowd dissipated without asking for any other proof from me. I had a sense of relief and thanked God that I could save the lives of two innocent beings who had lost virtually everything in the communal riots. It took some days for things to settle down in the city. Arunima's mental condition was deteriorating and she became uncontrollable at times. I had to take her to a therapist, and she recovered from her depression for the sake of Pari. I had to bring them with me.

'Though I had to reconcile with my fate, but my heart was not letting me do so. The first thing I did was to go to office and enquire about you, but by that time you had resigned. I also came to know that you had got married and were happy with your spouse. I could feel the vacuum created in my life and the only way out was to consider Arunima and Pari as my family, a responsibility assigned to me by God.

'Arunima was becoming emotionally dependent on me and then I had to tell her everything about you and me. She is an understanding person; She said, "Rajan, for me you are everything, your status is more than the status of god in my life, but under no circumstance would I force myself on you. If you want I can let you live alone also and I will wait for you till you have feelings for me so that we can share our lives happily."

'But I did not allow her to leave me and stay unprotected with a child in this merciless world. We decided to live together but she has given me my space to do whatever pleases me. The cloak of time has covered her painful memories. But, at times, her ghastly past tortures her and she becomes uncontrollable; she has nightmares of the tragedy her family faced. With the help of meditation sessions, she again comes to terms with her life. Every year, she has been doing so and she feels much better for days after the session. I had also started to compromise with the life that destiny had for me, but today after seeing you after such a long time I felt as if I had gone back to my past and got my lost days back.'

Rajan held both of Suman's hands in his and said, 'You cannot even imagine how it feels to act like a hero in real life. Arunima might be considering me a hero, but what all I had to bear, she can never understand!'

The touch of Rajan's hand healed her wounds. Suman felt that she was experiencing the warmth of the sun after a long chilling winter. She could see the reflection of her days spent with Rajan in the tears that fell on her hand. They both had gone back to the time when they were together dreaming to spend their life together.

Suman said, 'But I am quite happy for you because Arunima is a gem of a person. Remember, I had spoken to you about a friend of mine when I saw my cousin with the man who ditched Anu. It was Anu only. Secondly, you have proved your worth as a good human being, and it is a matter of pride for me that once I was madly in love with you. And now that love has changed into respect, the reverence for a person who is almost like a god in this world full of demons.'

Rajan said, 'Suman, I am a human being, and I don't want to become God. I want my love back. It was destiny that parted us and now it seems that god is showing some mercy to us by making us meet again. Arunima is settled now with Pari. I looked after both as my responsibility, but trust me, not a day passed that I did not miss you.'

'Rajan, it was not easy for me to forget you. It's my heart and eyes only that know the pain I underwent.'

'Suman, it was fate that swept us away to follow two different directions in life, but our luck has brought us together, once again.' Rajan looked into her eyes and said, 'Can't we leave the lives imposed on us and start afresh to have a life of our choice.'

Suman could not think of an answer instantly. She was quiet. And she moved out of the café saying, 'Rajan, it's time for the kids' bus to arrive.'

She left with Kusum without speaking a word to Rajan.

Suman was back with Kusum. This time she was less perturbed less due to Kunal and more due to her re-introduction to her past.

THIRTY-SIX

THE INTERNATIONAL CONFERENCE was hanging like a dagger over Kunal's head. The presentation in the offing could be the most eventful happening of his career. A lot depended on the results of the presentation. He fantasized about the improving bottom line of the company, the share value going up, and the man to whose effort all this would be credited would be him, Kunal. His name would be written with golden letters in the history of his company records.

But, Tara's absence in the conference raised many questions in his mind! Though Aditya was quite efficient and could assist him, and there hardly seemed any need for Tara to be present at the conference—yet because she had vanished from the scene in a very suspicious way, that caused the greatest worry to Kunal. He had asked Aditya to call her up after reaching Singapore also, but it was the same response "…not reachable…"

Kunal was tossing on his bed, when the doorbell rang. He sprang up from his bed thinking it must be Tara! His dying faith revived, and it brought a smile back on his face.

He slipped on the gown from the cupboard, unlocked the door and started tying the belt.The door opened, but it was Aditya who stood outside.

'Aditya, what happened? Anything urgent that has brought you here so early in the morning, or maybe you have some news from Tara?'

'Sir, how do you know that I am here to share some news about Tara?'

'I just guessed.'

'Come, Come in,' said Kunal, leading him towards the chairs kept at the other end of the room. 'So, she finally talked to you! Isn't it?'

'No sir, you will just not believe what I am about to tell you.'

Kunal became quite anxious, 'What? What has she done?'

'Sir, I had to buy a new SIM card to talk to my family, so I went out to a nearby market. After purchasing the card, I was walking back towards the hotel when I saw Tara sitting on the back seat of a car with a man whom I had never seen before. The car was waiting at the red signal.'

'You mean Tara is here in Singapore, but with a different person,' Kunal said, looking thoughtful.

'Aditya, it is quite possible that she was someone else, and not Tara.'

'No, I am sure she was Tara, because as I tried to get closer and exchange a smile, she turned her face away, pretending as if she had never seen me before. And before I could reach closer, the car had already moved.'

Kunal didn't know what to do, so he said, 'Aditya, we need to be there for the presentation in time. At the moment, we really can't do much on Tara's issue! Let this presentation be over and then we will plan as to what has to be done.'

The delegates were from different companies from all over the world. While checking the names of participating companies and their respective countries, Kunal noticed that there was one more Indian company listed as a participant.

And the two rows of chairs arranged around the round table started becoming occupied with the participants—the front ones closer to the table being for the person who had to make the presentation, while the back row was for their assistants helping them. Kunal had a shock when he saw Tara occupying the back row of chairs behind an Indian gentleman. Aditya whispered in Kunal's ears, 'Sir, this is the man I saw this morning with Tara.' Kunal nodded.

The companies had filed their submissions online, and based on the details mentioned in the proposal, the presentation was to be made for explaining the modus operandi and the specificity that could make the deal a profitable one for the international partner.

After the welcome speech, and the presentations by representatives of companies, the results were announced. And to Kunal's shock the deal went to the other Indian company Suvam Enterprises instead of KNC Ltd—Kunal's company.

There was a big round of applause for the winner; willingly or unwillingly everyone present had to join in the clapping. Hearing the name of Suvam Enterprises as the Indian company bagging the deal, the ground appeared to be sinking under Kunal's feet. He lifted the glass of water kept before him and gulped down the entire water in one go. His ears buzzed with the sound of the clapping reverberating in the hall.

Both Kunal and Aditya knew who was behind the success of Suvam Enterprises. The company joining as a last minute contender and winning the deal was not a miracle, but a well thought out plan of Tara. The proposal and the figures were copied from KNC Ltd with slight modifications, making it profitable for the International partners initially, but releasing great potential for Suvam Enterprises after one year. All the work was Kunal's, and Tara had stolen his entire effort and sold it to Suvam Enterprises at the price of a lucrative career and sizeable authority in the company.

After the announcement of the deal, the delegates were requested to join for high tea. Kunal sat on his chair feeling cheated, robbed and swindled by someone whom he had trusted. His head hung low with shame and disgrace; he wished the ground would swallow him up not because he had lost the deal, but because Tara had made a big fool of him.

Kunal told Aditya, 'I won't let her get off like this!' He wanted to settle scores with Tara. He wanted to rough her up, but Aditya restrained him from doing so, warning him of the grave consequences it could lead to!

A storm brewed inside Kunal. He told Aditya to find out the hotel where she was staying. Aditya enquired from the concierge of his hotel and he could dig out all the details of Tara's stay at Singapore.

Kunal and Aditya decided to shift to the hotel where Tara stayed. She was not back in her room and Kunal and Aditya went to the open bar near the swimming pool. It is rightly said that people drink not just to celebrate but also to overpower their grief. And Kunal was sinking in the agony that his misery was his own creation. He wanted to drink like a fish to swallow the bitter pill of treachery by someone whom he trusted.

Most of the employees at KNC Ltd had suffered at the hands of Tara in some form or other because she misused her clout with senior officials to trouble those lower down. And Aditya too had lots of grudges against her. He used the opportunity to vent his spleen to bring out Tara's dirty secrets before Kunal, though it was too late. Aditya narrated everything about Tara's background to Kunal.

Tara was a small town girl who had come to the city for pursuing her higher education. Her father was a rich kiln owner having a cement and brick business in the suburbs of Uttar Pradesh. She had never been keen on studies; it was mainly the attraction of a big town that she made her move to the metropolitan, by getting enrolled in a private vocational course.

In the big city, she had all the freedom to do whatever she wished. The late night parties and moving around with friends were her favorite pastimes. Her parents had no dearth of money. They had loosened their purse strings for their daughter. They used to think that their daughter's educational pursuit would enhance their family status.

When her actions started showing in the form of her

unsatisfactory results, and a warning letter was sent to her parents about Tara's conduct, her parents became worried. She was called back. They married her off to a well-educated boy, employed as an officer in a bank.

The marriage did not work because Tara was not the type of girl to adjust to her husband's limited income and to take up the responsibility of his old parents. All her energy and efforts were directed towards the maintenance of the glow and glamour of her body. She did not mind using this glow and glamour for earning favors, money and fame. She was not the kind to adhere to the rules and regulations of family life.

Nishant, Tara's husband, was a gentleman. He tried to fulfill his wife's wishes but her ever-increasing demands went beyond his means. He was the only support of his parents so he could not drive his parents into an old age home, at the behest of his wife. The initial tiffs took the form of serious clashes. Despite the entreaties of her husband and her in-laws, she applied for divorce and custody of her child.

Finally, Nishant and Tara settled for a divorce, with Tara taking charge of her son Saubhagya. She moved away from him by managing a job through her uncle.

Then, with her money and the influence of her parents, she took custody of the child, letting him meet his father only occasionally.

'Why did no one tell me about her before, Aditya?'

'But, sir, would you have heard me earlier? No one could dare to raise their voice against Tara, because of the rapport she shared with you, and in fact, with all our senior bosses.'

'What do you mean? Is she close to many people in our office?'

'No, she is close to power and money! Whosoever has greater access to it she is close to them,' Aditya said, in a voice full of sarcasm.

THIRTY-SEVEN

KUNAL AND ADITYA kept waiting for Tara and kept enquiring at the reception, but she was not back in her room till midnight. Next morning, Kunal got up with an empty feeling, his head heavy due to the previous night's drinks. The hangover of the drinks could not fill the emptiness in his heart. His blood boiled at the thought of being cheated and the loss to his company. He wanted to throttle Tara and take his revenge!

Without checking whether she was back in her room or not, he rushed out of his room and barged into Tara's room, finding its door ajar. Someone seemed to have just left.

Kunal skimmed through the cluttered room; the pillows were scattered on the floor, and the white bed sheet was crumpled. The table had two cocktail glasses, one empty and the other still containing traces of wine in it. The ashtray was full of cigarette stubs and the smell of tobacco mixed with the smell of wine still wafted across the room.

He was face to face with Tara in her déshabillé state. Her face looked discolored with the makeup worn off, and hair dishevelled. He was seeing her face sans make up for the first time, since he knew her. The skin under her eyes was wrinkled, and the spots on her face made her look different from how she normally looked.

Tara was wearing a cream color satin bodice gown. It had molded cups emphasized with frills, lace, and a transparent long skirt; she had made all efforts to make herself look hot. Kunal found her ugly.

She was caught unawares by Kunal coming into her room. She got up from the bed and said, 'You! What are you doing here?'

'You bloody bitch! I don't want to utter foul words to make my mouth dirty. I have already damaged myself a lot because of your company—the most obnoxious female.' Kunal had lifted the cocktail glass to throw at her, but then he stopped himself, with great difficulty.

'I am wrong to put you in the category of a human being; you are fit only to be called a bloody blood sucking witch! You kept playing games with me for making me a ladder for your career!' Kunal shouted.

'Kunal, it's enough! I won't take any more bullshit from you. And if you don't listen to me, I am calling up reception for help! And you, what are you? Don't you men suck your women by using them for as long you find them useful, and then throw them out for women like me? Because the truth is that you are also equally selfish! You want everything for your pleasure, enjoyment and to stroke your ego! And when a woman does it to you, your ego is hurt because men have all the liberty of having fun in life!'

'And, mind it, I am not a fool like your wife!'

'Don't you talk about my wife. You cannot compare yourself with her.'

'That's what I said just now that I am not a fool like her. An educated fool,' Tara shouted.

Tara was right in a way; Kunal was getting a taste of his own medicine. His tone became softer and he said, 'Tara don't talk about my family to prove that you are right! Have you ever thought about your son? Do you even bother to know how he is being taken care of? You have left him at the mercy of your maid.'

'What mercy! Now you have started bringing my personal life in our professional discussion, and since you have broached the topic, let me make things clear to you—I am giving my son whatever he needs. I earn only for him, to give him a good and comfortable life. Whatever I am doing is for him, for his happiness. I have given him all comforts of life; he has the best of toys, food and everything that an affluent child should have,' Tara said with aplomb.

Kunal stared at Tara. What a hypocrital lady she was! She had disguised her own pleasure seeking needs as the needs of her child. All the logic given by Kunal to arouse Tara's motherly instincts fell flat on its face.

'Look Kunal, it was quite a simple deal. I got a better deal with Suvam Enterprises so I joined them.'

Kunal was astounded to see Tara stoop to such an abysmal level. She had compromised all ethics, human values and sensitivity just for material gain.

'Tara, whatever said and done, I will drag you to the court for this. You have ruined our deal.'

'What!' Tara roared with laughter. 'Mr Kunal! under what law and with what proof? At the most, you will not clear my dues! I have already posted my resignation to the chief, and here is your copy.' She flung an envelope in the air which hit him on his face.

'And I don't even want any claims to be settled with your company because my one month's salary here is more than the six months' salary there including the dues and the perks—so please, thank you and get lost from my room. You have no right to enter my room without permission!'

It was like a hard slap on his face, which did not make

any sound but impacted his ego, esteem and self-respect.

With the feeling of defeat, treachery and insult, Kunal entered his room in the hotel. Wondering whether it was God's way of giving justice to his wife whom he had made to suffer because of this immoral lady, or was it his own wrongdoings whose outcome he had to face in the form of humiliation! His head felt terribly heavy; his misbehavior with Suman during the past few days filled him with remorse.

He could not even gather enough courage to make an apology to her.

"If she asks me the reason for the change in my behavior, what shall I say? Because a wicked lady has spurned me, I have come back to you! Will she trust me and give me another chance…?" Kunal was in conversation with himself.

He held his head in his hands and reached the table where water was kept. He poured water in a glass and his glance fell on the small blue kit kept in his bag; it was a medicine bag, which Suman had slipped in his clothes bag. It contained all the first aid medicines for headaches, loose motions, fever etc. Suman was very well aware of Kunal's careless nature. She knew his needs better than him. He opened the pouch and swallowed a tablet for headache. Now he would have to gear up to face the consequences for the loss his company had to bear because of losing the deal. He felt awful. At this moment, he realized the value of his family to him. This incident was a turning point in his life. He realized that his family was the base, the root which made his existence meaningful.

All the way to the airport, he kept thinking how he would face his wife and daughter, with whom he had been behaving so badly of late just because of Tara.

THIRTY-EIGHT

SUMAN'S DETERIORATING RELATIONS with Kunal for past few days had made her feel quite miserable. There was a lot of frustration building up within her. In fact, she had already decided to live separately from Kunal—then why not live with Rajan? If Kunal could choose somebody else for himself despite her utmost devotion, then she also had the right to choose a life in which she was happy, and nothing else could have made her life happier than staying with Rajan. She and Rajan had at one point of time decided to be life partners.

Next day Suman met Rajan at the bus stop.

She asked him, 'But who will look after Arunima and Pari?'

'Suman, let me tell you that Arunima and I are just sharing the premises, and nothing more than that. We are still almost like strangers for each other. Maybe Arunima is waiting for the day I will have some feelings for her, and then we shall get into a better relationship. She has hopes that I will accept her as my wife one day, but Suman I will not be able to do justice to her knowing fully well that you are around. Also, I can care for them even while being away. And may be, by being away from me she will be able to think of having some other person in her life. I will shift my base to Mauritius. The office here and of Mauritius are under my charge these days. Mauritius is my second home. I have a bungalow and a complete establishment there.'

Rajan's proposal breathed fresh life into Suman and she agreed to it!

'But what will happen to Kusum, Rajan? I cannot leave Kusum with Kunal. I will bring her along with me.'

Rajan agreed. 'Suman, I love you, and when I say that I mean to accept you completely. Kusum is a part of you, and I know you cannot stay away from her. Of course, you are going to bring her with you.'

Rajan's words pacified her, and she felt completely at peace.

She wanted to give Kunal a reason for leaving him. She wanted to leave with a clear conscience by making Kunal realize that it was his infidelity that made her take this step because she also had a right to her happiness, like him. And she was not betraying him, nor insulting him, like he had done. Suman told Rajan that they would wait for Kunal and Arunima to be back, and Rajan agreed.

The school bus arrived and both Suman and Rajan took charge of their kids and headed towards their homes.

Suman started to imagine her life with Rajan. She tried to feel happy imagining herself with him but each time she did so she felt she had to cross the Rubicon of her family life. Suman tried justifying herself. Kunal was responsible for this extreme step of hers. He had threatened her world of happiness by bringing a person like Tara into their life. She shoved aside all thoughts of him which were coming in the way of her new life with Rajan. After all, I am responsible for my own self; I have every right to be happy. After trying hard, she could settle the rising ripples of thoughts in her mind.

She had so much to do before leaving her house; pack Kusum's and her clothes, sort out and organize bank documents of her account which still had all her salary in it. She thought of taking away the jewellery she had received as a gift in her marriage because she did not want Tara to touch anything that had her beautiful memories preserved in them.

Each time she packed a set of clothes, a piece of jewellery, her certificate etc. the associated memories flooded her mind. The saris her mother bought for her marriage and the occasions when she wore them—each dress started telling her the story of good times she had spent with Kunal. With great difficulty she was able to pack her clothes, strengthening herself against the onslaught of emotions, which made only women weaken their resolve.

"Why don't men fall prey to such emotions when they know that their lady has invested everything she had for their happiness?" She decided that she was intellectually as capable as her husband and she would not give in to such weakening emotions.

Rajan had booked open flight tickets for Mauritius. Suman had decided to leave the very next day after Kunal was back from his South Asia tour.

Suman was impatiently waiting for him to arrive. She was also rehearsing the lines she would speak to him before leaving the house. Apprehending that the words may fail her, she had also written a letter for Kunal telling him the reason for leaving him.

THIRTY-NINE

KUNAL REACHED HIS house full of remorse, penitence, and guilt for his deeds. It was after the loss of the international deal when the chickens had come home to roost, that he had known the value of small things in life which make up a home. Where even the smallest of one's need is taken care of; the minutest of one's feelings can be expressed without fear or insecurity of incurring anyone's wrath. He had been away for just a week, but it felt that he was back home after a long exile.

He pressed the bell with some effort. He was feeling tired. He felt devastated emotionally with the guilt of mistreating Suman.

Kusum opened the door for him. He had lost the deal, but a soft and beautiful garland of the small arms of his daughter encircled his neck. The warm kisses of the young cherub suffused his face and forehead to obliterate all marks of dejection from his spirits. She was shouting, 'Papa! Papa!'

It sounded sweeter than honey to his ears, better than the accolades received on winning a deal. He had forgotten everything that happened in Singapore. He had reached his heaven, his home.

Suman had also come out of the kitchen. She was putting all the containers in order so that the new person in the kitchen could easily work without wasting time looking for ingredients. She was thinking, "Kunal will surely miss me for the food, because I had perfected my cooking to suit his taste."

But why was she concerned when she was leaving him? She should let the things be, rather than being bothered about them. But she wanted to end her relationship with Kunal on a happy note. She had a smile on her face. There was no grudge, anger or any mark of embitterment. Rajan, by then, had got the tickets confirmed for the next available flight to Mauritius.

Kunal made Kusum sit in his lap. He kept listening to her nursery rhymes and stories in her babbling baby tone. Kunal attentively listened to all of Kusum's chatter, sometimes singing with her and at others smiling and clapping. Kusum went on and on to grab the attention of her father, till she became exhausted and dozed off in

Kunal's arms. She was holding his hand all the while as if she feared being separated from her father again. Kunal's week long absence from the house had made her apprehensive.

Kunal looked like a changed man to Suman. She could see Kunal as he was in their initial days after marriage. Then, she distracted herself lest her resolve to be with Rajan became weak. She would stick to her decision of getting her happiness back.

All this while, Suman was framing words to speak her mind to Kunal, but she was not able to get the right words to begin the conversation. Before Suman could find the right words to start speaking, Kunal spoke, 'I'm sorry Suman.'

'What!'

Suman was not prepared for this. The word 'sorry' created a big hurdle in speaking her mind to Kunal.

She was not in a position to respond to him. Nothing came out from her mouth; yes, or no, or any complaints or grievances—nothing!

The word 'sorry' from Kunal made an impact, like a stone creating ripples in standing water, but the memories of the party night flashed in her mind and the pain made her heart ache. She did not want to listen to Kunal. Suman didn't know why he was a changed man and for how long he would remain so?

She got up from her seat and tried moving away from him for fear that it would foil her plans of going with Rajan! But Kunal held her hand and pleaded with her to sit beside him. He requested, 'Suman, a sorry is not enough for my behavior, but I have already had the punishment for ill-treating you.'

Suman looked at his face. He held her hand but kept his eyes low, not looking directly at her, as a lost soul who would collapse if he did not get her support.

'What happened?' Suman asked tersely. The anger of the party day could not be smothered, but she managed to keep a tab on her emotions by concealing them under forced coquettishness.

'Why are you looking so upset? I hope you are feeling fine,' she asked. But to Kunal, Suman's tone did not matter. He just wanted her next to him!

He confessed everything to Suman. From the day he developed a soft corner for Tara, to the day of his betrayal. 'Suman, I have not been fair to you, but please forgive me.'

Suman did not want to be rude to Kunal, but she had decided to move out of his life with Rajan, who was waiting for her with the dreams of a beautiful future. This time she was not able to look into Kunal's eyes; she was thinking that it was too late, but still she was not able to utter anything to him about her plans.

Kunal said, 'Suman, I am very tired. I want to sleep.'

'Ok,' said Suman.

Kunal slipped inside the covers next to Kusum. Father and daughter slept carelessly without any inkling of what was in store for them. Kusum's hand rested on Kunal's chest. Suman opened her cupboard to take out the purse to put the keys in it.

Suddenly, the landline phone started ringing. She had set the ringer's tone low so that Kusum did not wake up cranky due to the phone.

'Who could this be in the middle of the night?' Suman spoke in a low tone. Her heart wrenched with an unknown fear; phone calls at odd hours had often been for communicating some bad news. Before the sound of the phone reached anyone else she rushed to grab the receiver.

It was her mother calling.

'Hello!' Savita's voice came from the other end.

'Ma, what happened? Is everything all right?' Suman asked hurriedly to still the waves of fear mounting within her.

'Yes, everything is fine. But Suman?'

'What Ma?' Though Suman's fear was allayed but she became more anxious to know the sentence after but…

'Suman,' said Savita, 'I just called up to check—is everything fine? Actually, I had a very bad dream and was feeling quite uneasy, so I called up to check your well-being!'

She asked about Kunal and Kusum and said, 'Take good care of Kunal, Kusum and yourself. We will visit India shortly and stay with you for a few days.'

Suman said, 'Ma, you are worrying unnecessarily; everything is fine here.' She could not utter a word about what she was up to! Had her mother called up even an hour later, she would have been with Rajan. And that one moment could have changed the course of her life, and of all the persons connected to her. A sense of guilt started overpowering her.

She sank on the chair next to the phone and started thinking about her decision. She again looked at Kunal and Kusum having no inkling of what was going on in Suman's mind.

After talking to her mother, her mind was full of questions! She was being tried in her own court. "Will Kusum be as comfortable with Rajan as she is with her father? What havoc was she going to cause in Arunima, her best friend's life?" Instead of being her support, she was taking away her only source of happiness, Rajan.

"Mom and Dad will be here, and I will be with Rajan, in Mauritius! Oh my god, what am I going to do? What a disgrace it will be for my family? To bring happiness in my life, I cannot ruin the lives of all my dear ones! I'm sure Mom would have had a heart attack listening to my plan. How did I take this immature decision? Am I not being selfish, dragging Kusum to a life which might spoil the innocence of her childhood? Wouldn't Kusum miss her father and question my decision? Even if I am Kusum's mother, what right have I to spoil my daughter's life?" Mothers sacrifice their lives for the children rather than making children sacrifice for theirs! Suman was in a fix! She was unable to decide what to do?

She realized that Rajan and her feelings for him might not have changed in all the years gone by, but they both had walked great distances in their lives. And now their paths were set widely apart. If they both tried to make their paths meet, it would mean traversing of paths and trampling lives of people who had becoame associated with them in the course of their journeys. However, she and Rajan may try, but they could not go back to their past and make a new start.

She was in conversation with her conscience and it said, "Love is the nectar of life, but if the same love becomes poison for lives of others then it is better to sacrifice that love rather than spread poison in other's lives."

She remembered that even her mom and dad used to fight, but did either of them think of breaking up the family due to the fight—would she and her siblings have had the life that was full of happiness and emotional security.

The incident of the party again flashed before her eyes. She shuddered with indignation. Her conviction started becoming feeble. Kunal had hurt her self-esteem. And what was the guarantee that he would not behave badly with her again?

"But Suman, it is your life, and you are responsible for your actions? For Kunal's mistakes, you are going to punish your daughter, your parents, your best friend! Shouldn't you try to save your family for their sake? For Kunal's behavior he should be responsible and is feeling remorse for doing wrong." Suman's conscience was again talking

Did her worth depend on Kunal alone, whether he acknowledged her as good or bad? She may have lost her importance for Kunal, but then what about Kusum for whom her parents were the entire world. Then her parents, who derived their happiness from seeing their children happily settled in their homes.

Suman was thinking "Why should I gauge myself as per Kunal's standards? Who was Kunal to set a standard for her, when he could not fulfill his responsibility of a husband and a father?"

She was just not a wife; she also had the responsibility of being a mother, daughter, a good human being and a loyal friend.

She could not sacrifice the happiness of so many people and choose a life which suited her and Rajan just to prove her worth to Kunal. Even though she would not be with Rajan, his place in her life would never change. Rather, after knowing Arunima's story she had started adoring Rajan all the more. Maybe, if Rajan knew that she would not leave her family for the sake of her own happiness, he would think of accepting Arunima and Pari in his life as his family.

It was the moment of decision in Suman's life. Her one decision could affect the lives of so many people. She could not be selfish.

She started feeling giddy. She saw the flashlight of her mobile kept next to her purse blinking. She raced to check it. It had a message from Rajan. Their flight was to take off at 4 am, so they needed to leave right then, without any further delay.

'Suman, I am waiting outside your lift. Come fast or we might miss our flight.' He had sent a message earlier also, when he got into the cab. Now, he had sent the second message after he reached near her home to help her manage the luggage, and Kusum.

Suman looked at the message, waited for a while, and took a deep breath.

She wrote a text message, 'Rajan, I'm sorry. But we need to change our plans. I cannot come with you. Arunima and

Pari need you more than me. We will be friends forever. It will make me more than happy that I have such a good friend in you.'

Rajan was surprised to receive the message. He wrote again, 'Suman, any problems? Do you need help?'

Suman wrote, 'Rajan please go back to Arunima and Pari. They deserve to be with you. I think they deserve to have you in their life, and not me. Our families need us.'

Kunal was shaking Suman who had dozed off on the chair. 'Suman…Suman...What happened? Why have you packed the suitcase? Where are you going?'

Suman forced her eyes open. Her eyes felt heavy, but her heart and mind felt light, as she did not have any guilt feelings.

Her lips stretched into a smile uttering a lie for the benefit of all, 'I was going to Meerut to tell about your misbehaviour to Ma, your mom.'

'Suman, I am sorry. I promise that I will never misbehave again. Please don't leave me. You and Kusum are my world and I cannot live without you.' He kneeled before Suman and kept his head on her lap.

Suman put her hand on Kunal's head as a sign of assurance. She thanked god and her mother for making things fall in place at the right time.